Margaret of the Imperfections

Stories

Lynda Sexson

Persea Books
New York

Copyright © 1988 by Lynda Sexson

All rights reserved.

For information, contact the publisher:

Persea Books, Inc.
60 Madison Avenue
New York, New York 10010

Library of Congress Cataloging in Publication Data

Sexson, Lynda.
    Margaret of the imperfections.

    I. Title.
PS3569.E8857M36   1988   813'.54   88-4150
ISBN 0-89255-131-3
ISBN 0-89255-147-X (pbk.)

Designed by Peter St. John Ginna
Set in Zapf by Keystrokes, Lenox, Massachusetts
Printed and bound by Haddon Craftsmen, Scranton, Pennsylvania

First paperback printing, 1989

Acknowledgments

Acknowledgment is made to publications in which the following stories first appeared: "Starlings, Mute Swans, a Goose, an Impossible Angel, Evening Grosbeaks, an Ostrich, Some Ducks, and a Sparrow," *The Kenyon Review*; "Chalk Line," *The South Carolina Review*; "The Apocalypse of Mary the Unbeliever," in slightly different form, *Story Quarterly*; "Intestate and Without Issue," *High Plains Literary Review*; "When the Pie Was Opened," *Carolina Quarterly*; "Hope Chest," *Calliope*; "Margaret of the Imperfections," *The Kenyon Review*. I am grateful to the Djerassi Foundation and to Carl Djerassi. My deepest thanks to Michael. And I am grateful to Devin, Vanessa, Mother, Tom, Sue, Sarah, Karen, and Fred.

For my grandfather

Contents

Starlings, Mute
Swans, a Goose, an
Impossible Angel,
Evening Gros-
beaks, an Ostrich,
Some Ducks, and
a Sparrow

A WOMAN WEARING A BIB APRON AND carrying a man's humped lunch bucket walked past the window and Clay mistook her for an angel. She had a heavy step for an angel, but Clay leaned into the night to watch her turn left onto Alderson Street and play the lunch bucket across the Hemingways' picket fence. It was a racket the nosy neighbors claimed the next day not to have heard. Clay said it was just for him.

Before that singular event he had been indistinguishable from other thirteen-year-olds. I would have noticed; a year and a half younger and still planning to get discovered into Hollywood, I looked for signs of not only my potential beauty but anything in the house, the folks, even my brother that the biographers would be able to use—signs that would go unnoticed by common people, but sure childhood indications of my star quality. My brother wasn't worth any notice on the small list I kept for the convenience of my future historian, but Clay did know about it, and did his best to help me compile it.

Clayton, even then, was good to me, so when I tried to argue him out of his angel it was only because I didn't want him to go crazy on me.

That was twenty-seven years ago, and I remembered it all so easily when Clay called. In a man's voice he called up with a boy's claim: "Evelyn, can you come down for a couple of days?"

"Not without leaving several people and Auburn Public Library embarrassingly helpless. What do you need, Clayton?"

"I'd just like to see you." He dropped something against the phone. "It's the angel." He laughed like a boy; "I guess you'd say I've seen my angel again."

"How could it be the same one?" I stupidly challenged. And in the silence I began to make a list of things I had to take care of before I could drive down to see Clay. "I should be there by eight tomorrow night, but give me 'til ten. If it gets later, I'll call."

"Thanks, Evelyn. I can't wait for you to meet her."

"What'd you do, grab her and put her on a leash?"

"I want your blessing, sister."

"You have an angel in your backyard and you ask for a blessing from a sender of past-due notices?"

"You do remember that time I saw the angel, don't you?"

"Of course, Clay, I remember. I'll bring you something."

"I hope it's to eat and not to read."

"Fat and Illiterate: But an Angel Loved Him." I pretended a movie poster and appreciated Clay's snorty chuckle. A good brother, still polite enough to laugh at jokes too thin for most people to acknowledge hearing.

How odd it was, I thought as Clay said good-bye, that summer while I had been making my lists, getting my stardom down on lined paper, Clay said he was going to be a shepherd, imagining his adulthood as a boy's solitary campout. He ended up with a small-town theater, as close as I ever got to the movies; I never got beautiful and I never stopped making lists.

The kids, all three hovering around the ages we had been that summer, promised to keep track and check off the reminders I'd posted for each of them on the refrigerator. Bright enough, good, but somehow I could never imagine anything special in their lives, not as special as Clay and I had—well, I mean something like the intrusion of an angel. Maybe it's their ages, the sizes of them now, that caused me to have been dwelling upon that summer. Clay's call really didn't surprise me. I hadn't been able to get that summer out of my mind.

Alex balked. "If your brother's going off his rocker, I don't know that you can handle it. You've been a little nervous lately."

"Something's very important or he wouldn't have asked me to come."

"Evelyn, there are no angels. Angels don't exist."

"I know that. I'm sure Clay does, too. That's why he needs me. It's harder on nonbelievers when angels appear."

"Now you're off your rocker. Evvy, it was just his way of telling you he's in love. He didn't mean there's an angel, he meant there's a woman."

I gave him his list to follow in my absence, called Sue to make arrangements for the library, packed, remembering to include my surprise for Clayton, and made love with Alex in front of the fireplace to console him—both of us. Alex has never accepted the way a sister feels about her brother; he's always a little jealous of Clay.

I worried about Clay as I lay awake waiting for morning light so I could get going to Stoddard Hills. I hadn't slept much for weeks, it gave me the time I needed to align carefully everything in my world. Alex was right, seeing an angel was more ominous in a man nearly forty than in a thirteen-year-old boy. Maybe it would be too much for me. No, I thought, I'm all that Clay has; I would bear up. But it was easier for me that first time, too. What would I do if I should see—an angel—now? As Alex didn't know, and Clay never seemed to notice, I too had seen the angel that first time. I suppose it wasn't so important, as it was Clay's angel. Once in a while, though, I'd ask myself why I had seen her too.

"It's not an angel," I had protested then. "No feathers."

"She doesn't show her wings," he had said dreamily.

"She's a woman in an old cotton dress."

"And an apron," Clay agreed.

"Clay," I had whispered, "you don't even believe in God; you told me so."

"Of course I don't believe in God."

"Then you can't believe in angels."

"It seems like it. I wonder why she came." Clay has continued to be capable of agreeing with another's logic and affirming his own experience, no matter how disparate or contradictory.

I tried another point, "Angels wouldn't just walk by; they'd come and say something to you, like 'Behold' or 'Watch Out.'"

"Seems like it," Clay agreed again.

So we decided to sit up all night in case she returned, but we woke up sticky in the late morning heat. All that day we searched. I kept my spiral notebook with me.

On the way down, I kept thinking about how surprised Clay would be to see that old notebook. In fact, when I stopped to get him some Danish cherry cheese, a box of Baci, and some oranges with thick skins (because of his preference for the inner rind), I took the notebook out of my bag and put it on the car seat beside me. Should I have wrapped it? No, then he might misunderstand, I thought.

I glanced at it as I took the freeway to Stoddard. The page headed EVIDENTS brought back the route we had followed that next day. Only the trail of an angel made the weather bearable, and looking at the smeared page, I could feel once more the pencil sliding in my sweaty fingers as I had listed:

in front of house. feather.

Clay wanted me to write "not from a bird," but instead I put:

brown, pinkish tip.

black mark all the way a long on Hemingway fence.
But everyone we asked had heard no clatter the evening before.

I asked Mr. Hemingway how that black smudge got all across his fence. He narrowed his eyes toward Clay and said, "Dunno, but whoever did it must want to paint fences this summer." I wrote:

neighbors know nothing.

We followed Alderson Street, naming the residents, each house too modest for an angel, even a female, working-class angel. We let Toby sniff the feather and told him to find her. He led us to the creek, waded in and drank from it, shook and showered us, wagged his tail and panted. Clay insisted I note:

dogs cannot smell angels.

"Can't do it, Clayton," I had announced, sticking my pencil into the spiral. "Angels can't be found out like this— or every house would have one instead of a wife or a dog."

"Okay," said Clay. "When she comes back we'll be ready."

"How do you know she'll come back?"

"Because she's an angel."

Stoddard, in those days, was too small for anyone to pass by without a name, a point of origin, and a destination. An unknown woman walking our streets was about as likely as the appearance of a celestial being. I've often wondered how Clay could continue to live in the same town, in the house that we grew up in, sleep, my God, in the same big old brass bed he'd had as a boy, walk the same seven blocks to work every morning.

Old Mrs. Grabow whimsically had bequeathed him the movie house, chandeliers, dusty plush, plaster-of-paris baroque and all, when Clay was twenty-two and facing adulthood empty-handed—and empty-headed too, as I remember. Her attorney said she had held some notion that Clay would have charmed the pants off her aunt Marcella, for whom the theater had been named. When I used to unwrap my money to trade for those Saturday pictures, I had no idea the Marcella I sat in was really an idealization of Mrs. Grabow's aunt; not having to be content with a mere tombstone to commemorate her turning back round to dust, she became a local goddess of the movie reel. Clay took to the Marcella without hesitation, but to my mind, without ever really making a decision either. He catered to his own eccentric tastes, allowing little theater to push aside his favorite reruns each summer and managed, by accident I think, to get people coming in from three nearby college towns to his Marcella, now known as an art house. Dad was pretty hurt Clay didn't want to mix concrete and spread blacktop for him. But Mom said he didn't have to be "Sand, Gravel, and Son;" of course her family was made up of pale schoolteachers, a cranky judge, and a lady who fainted at the sound of trains.

But he never moved; he never married. Clay, I guess, still wouldn't make anyone's list as a notable person, except once he saw an angel. Twice now? I wondered. Had he really seen it again? Impossible. Did I read somewhere that *impossible* is another word for *the inevitable*, which avoids commitment to a cosmic time schedule? No, if I did read it, I wouldn't remember it; it wouldn't have made any sense until now. Although there was something like that—in a gardening manual I shelved the other day, I think.

Why couldn't—I realized as my body wilted with the driving and my mind quickened with the concentrated energy of memory—why couldn't the angel reappear? After all, she had come more than once, even then.

We gave up our quest that long-ago day and went home to tuna fish and lemonade, and Clay convinced me that the angel would return.

I finally said, trying to be something more than an accessory to the drama, with my movie star pauses and intonations, " . . . the real mystery, my child, is the angel's lunch bucket."

"No, the mystery's the angel." But he was snared; "What do you think's in it?"

"Liverwurst and coffee," I said maliciously.

"Not in an angel's lunch bucket! And if you say any more things like that, I won't let you see her with me." He almost cried.

Inexplicably, I did cry. I was so embarrassed, I claimed to Mom that he'd punched me. We endured her harangue about how we should get along better while the afternoon heated up even into the pantry and we waited to get back to the business of the angel.

Then Clay and I went out and sat in the creek and watched the neighbor's ducks abandon the big pond Mr. MacNab had spent three years making to join us in the sluggish creek. Aggie MacNab, Mom used to like to say—she must have told the story a hundred times—had badgered her Stanley for years to make her a "sizable lake out back of the house." Mom would imitate Aggie's whine; Mom must have wanted to be in the movies, too. Since there was nothing but brushy wood and lumps of land Clay and I called our mountains, Stanley worked with a red and puffy face to realize his wife's vision. "None of us"—Mom used to giggle for company—"had any idea what she was really after. When that big pond, Fake Lake," she'd say, stealing our name for it, "was finished, and a really pretty enough thing, Aggie sent off mail-order for a couple of big eggs. She hatched them out. Mute swans. Lord, I hate to think what they cost. We named them Nest and Egg," she laughed. Really it was Dad who had christened them. "When poor

Stanley found out how much they cost he refused to look
at them. They revenged him by considering his pond in-
adequate"—she pronounced each syllable of the word as
though she were reading it from a dictionary—"and they
up and died. First one and then the other, things that couldn't
make a peep." Mother always found that part especially
funny, that the swans were mute.

I didn't ever think the story was amusing, because I
remember the three things that went together. First, I was
the one who found them and showed Aggie, and she said,
"Look how they died in each other's arms." It didn't look
like that to me. They looked dirty and looked like their necks
were broken. The ducks walked back and forth as though
they didn't even notice. It was, I think, the next day that
Stanley fell over in his welding shop and left Aggie a widow
with a "sizable lake out back of the house." That was the
second thing. Right after that Mrs. Grabow ordered a goose
sent to Aggie. Harold Hemingway, who ran Mrs. Grabow's
errands, didn't realize she meant a roast goose to express
sympathy over Stanley; he thought she meant a live one to
replace the loss of those ugly, half-grown swans. The goose
was the third thing. Mom said it was the last straw. "That
goose is the last straw," she said and made Dad and Clay
clutch their sides laughing. "No," said Dad, "that goose is
Cookie." Clay and Dad had talked Aggie into naming the
goose Cookie, which she said was a sweet enough name.
They howled when they came in the back door, 'til they fell
into each other's arms. I'd never seen anything like it. Clay
explained to me, until tears ran down Dad's cheeks, that
"It's Stanley's goose that's cooked; the goose's goose didn't
get cooked; the goose is still cookin'." I'd never seen Dad be
so silly, and he'd known Stanley for years—even liked to
help him work on that pond. God, it was that same summer.
Just before we went for the angel's lunch bucket.

On one of the pages in the old notebook, Clay had
drawn a map. By the time he'd made Fake Lake, the Moun-

tains, the Creek, he had to crowd everything else together. I had trouble understanding the arrows, but I was ready to do my part in capturing the lunch bucket.

After the supper that everyone was too hot to eat, we sneaked Dad's lunch bucket from the drainboard and waited behind the ancient maple that our arms never did grow long enough for the two of us to encircle. She came along, all right, swinging her lunch bucket at her side. We jumped from behind the tree and stood blocking the sidewalk.

The angel looked straight at us. She looked just like a real woman except her skin was missing a layer—she looked peeled.

Clay made a face, hoping his practiced ferocity would cause her to drop her lunch bucket, which we would surreptitiously exchange for our father's ordinary lunch bucket, exactly like her ideal one. She didn't startle; she didn't budge. I flew back to our place behind the tree. Clay was left unprotected, facing down his angel on the sidewalk. He let out a sound like water going down the drain, grabbed the angel's lunch bucket from her, dashed around the tree, wrenched Dad's from my petrified, clenched fist, ran back to the angel, thrusting at her what he hoped she'd think was her own lunch bucket.

The woman snickered, and took off walking, swinging her arms and Dad's lunch bucket.

I followed Clay back through the porch window into my room. He set the lunch bucket on the cedar chest and we crouched on the floor in front of it. Neither of us moved to open it.

Finally, unable to stay near it, we retreated to Clay's room. He let Toby and me share his bed, making it all the hotter that night. Early the next morning, Mom screamed from the kitchen, "What'd you kids do with your daddy's lunch pail?"

If I had to count the most heart-stopping moments of my life, they'd all be clustered in those few days of that one summer. We dressed and dashed to my room; without pausing, Clay unsnapped the lid and I tipped the contents out onto my cedar chest. Clay snapped the pail shut and ran it to Mom.

"What were you doing with it?" she was quizzing, but Clay was already back with me, staring at what the angel had kept in her lunch bucket. We had never seen such things: sugared violets, rose petals, and mint leaves, spilling from their wax-paper protections; they were so beautiful, I found myself crying again.

"It's what she eats," Clay whispered. After great deliberation, I decided to eat them myself. Clay wouldn't touch them. "I'll live forever and you'll die," I told him.

"Let's give some to Toby and see what happens to him."

"No," Clay objected, "we shouldn't give angel food to dogs."

So I ate them and Clay watched. And Dad unknowingly packed his sandwiches to his Ready-Mix and Paving in an angel's lunch bucket.

For years after, when Dad would happily complain about Clay growing so fast and threaten to put a brick on his head, I'd think someone was going to find out why I remained so scrawny. Clay really did grow into a good-looking man; I guess I should have abstained from the confections. Once I discovered candied flowers in a specialty shop, when I was still in college. I sent some to Clay. He didn't answer. He didn't answer any of my letters; but maybe even then he was not amused to confess we'd fooled ourselves into an imaginary angel; but now he was ready to turn around and admit she was real.

I must have driven faster than I intended; it was still daylight when I pulled into the driveway. The lilacs were fully out, although some were beginning to rust. I got out of the car, and there was a sudden rush and beating of wings, something hurting me, a hideous noise. All I could think was that the angel was there guarding the house and was going to kill me rather than let me near Clay.

Clay lifted me off the car fender, laughing. "Go away, Cookie," he said, and the old goose waddled off. "It's okay, Evvy; it's just Cookie, Aggie's old goose. He's not even well; he must really love you to work up such a greeting." It couldn't be the same goose; the damn thing couldn't live that long, plaguing me since that summer I can't shake from my consciousness. Clay hugged me tightly, until I pushed him away.

In the old days Clay could punch me, or I could jump him. Now we go for months, sometimes a year without seeing each other, and I can tell, he feels as I do, wanting to do some mild violence to each other, just to say hello. As it is, we've never mastered a mature, comfortable sibling greeting. So, I immediately leapt to the reason why I'd come—to save him from an angel. I loaded him up with packages and confronted him with my first reasonable objection: "Clay, if it were the same woman, she'd have to be nearly seventy years old."

"Unless she were the same angel," he teased, "then she'd certainly be much, much older." He was silly, almost giddy.

In the house, she was waiting for me. He called her Muriel; I saw that it was she. What was this monster doing in Clay's house? I thought she'd look as though she slept with hot-water bottles and played the dulcimer, but she wore a knotted scarf for a belt over loose, printed, silk shirt, vest, and skirt, like a magazine idea of country costume, so many shades of pink, red, and purple in the various prints, I was distracted. Clay had hardly introduced me to her when he rushed my things to my room, leaving us alone.

Before her silence seeped into my skin, I asked her, casually as though she were an authentic and reasonable guest, "Does your family come from around here? What is it that they do?" It sounded accusatory rather than conversational; I started to perspire, or perhaps it was the moist atmosphere she emitted, pressing against me.

"Oh, I come from a fine old extinguished family." She

didn't smile. It seemed as though she had memorized responses for any stock question, but like a child (or an alien) the language was not quite hers and she garbled the meaning with approximated sound.

She bent to rearrange the fading narcissus blossoms in Mom's old Roseville vase. She gave them a final pat and they looked freshly cut again. Then she looked at me. I realized then that it had been an intended joke, her extinguished family. Was she, my God, referring to the Fall of Lucifer, his light extinguished; or worse, was she making a joke on the Death of God? I felt heat pressing up against the back of my neck. I thought for a moment that something was going wrong with me, but I knew I was too organized ever to go mad. The dry bloom she had removed from the bouquet rattled like cellophane when she crumpled it in her hand. With my senses intact, and my attention to mundane detail, I knew from the things I had scanned in the BF section of the library that I was a substantial distance from insanity; I was acutely aware of each detail of Muriel's activity.

"What's this?" asked Clay, returning and optimistic that he might be interrupting a conversation.

"Evelyn was just asking me about my family." She smiled toward Clay.

"The last thing any normal person would want to gab about," he said, laughing.

I turned away from them, surprised not at the sudden rush of tears, but at how hot they felt in the rims of my eyes.

"You just relax from your long drive," she announced. "I'll have dinner soon."

"Oh, Muriel," said Clay. "Evelyn brought these to you: looks like oranges, Danish cheese, and hazelnut kisses."

"For me? How thoughtful," she said like old dialogue. She turned me toward her. "Thank you, Evelyn. And thank you so much for taking the time to come and meet me."

Muriel didn't look very old, but her face looked as though her youth had been accidentally rubbed off into the pillow while she slept; but it was a face that was incapable of attracting the careful, detailed craftsmanship of old age— of a life lived. It was like my doll Miranda's face, which unmistakably reflects the years without ever changing its features or complexion; Miranda sits the years in the cedar chest, without sun or season, but whenever Katie would pack her around for a day or two, calling her "Momma's Old-anda," the doll in my daughter's arms was reminiscent of the old photographs of me, renewed, given flesh and spirit; yet Miranda ruined the picture, she was a *memento mori*, time-marred and time-reminding. When Kate outgrew her interest, I'd occasionally retrieve Miranda myself and look at her placid face, always the same, but mysteriously marking the years. To look at my doll was like first looking at Muriel; she was pulling some knotted thread out of my tightening memory. Muriel, like Miranda, looked exactly like Clay's angel, no changes but for the invisible, inevitable shadow of nearly thirty years. I looked at her and instead of saying something gracious, I protested, "Coincidence."

Muriel bent close to my face to encourage my voiceless words. Strands of her hair caught in my dumb mouth; she wound her hair into a spring and pushed it behind her ear, smiling a "Bless you." Her smell was so familiar and so sudden, it rocked me. It was not the powder and perspiration scent of the widows who graze the library, the women who usually bent so close to me with their smiles and blessings. Muriel had the thick, lustrous hair of a fourteen-year-old girl, like Kate's, but she didn't smell like her. What was that scent about her that seemed to belong to me? I looked at her face, still close. I didn't listen to what she was saying. Instead of the relief map of worn skin, she looked like a peeled Easter egg, pulled moist from the shell and stained with traces of the dye. The odor increased, almost as if she were talking to me through that sense. Then I suddenly knew: it was the smell of that night. I didn't even remember it; how could she know about it?

That night penetrated my knowledge; Clay had persuaded my mother to let him sleep out. I maneuvered her into permitting him only if he let me too. He put up the tent out by the trees and turned it into a playhouse while I was off at my piano lesson.

I even remember what I was working on then; I had worked on it for two months—Bach's first prelude from *The Well-Tempered Clavier*. Mrs. Grabow, rarely satisfied with me, had said, "They heard you in heaven." She hugged me. (And she smelled of perspiration and powder.) For a moment I believed her; my fingers tingled and I was afraid.

Clay met me coming home. He had his water pistol; it was so hot, I held up my hair and he shot the back of my neck. We took turns drinking from it, aiming the barrel into each other's mouths, squirting the warm, plastic-tinged water.

The tent was remote from the house. The canvas walls glowed in the sunlight; we sat in it 'til we felt we would suffocate.

"Did Mrs. Grabow ever tell you they heard you in heaven?"

"Yeah," said Clay, "she says that all the time."

"She only said it to me once."

Night resisted for hours, and then surprised us. I pulled my old army-surplus mummy bag out of the tent, insisting I would watch the three or four stars that had showed up. Clay stayed in his tent because he had set it up. We whispered 'til we slept. I awoke to rain and lay there for some moments in the downpour, too surprised and disoriented to move. I finally crawled into the tent, pulling the heavy, wet bag along.

"Clay. I'm cold. I'm all wet." He opened his bag and I got in. He was hot and dry; our bodies met with a wonderful awkward compensation.

I lay there, smelling the wet down bag, Clay's hot, sweet arm, the cool rain. I watched through the tent opening the silent lightning limp beyond the town and stumble back toward us. I smelled the lightning, too, or else something located in my elbows. I meant to forget that time.

That next morning Mom had put calamine lotion on my bug bites and made us disassemble the tent. "No more," she had said. So we languished all day in the heat until, yes, it was—it was that very next night that Clay's angel had come down the sidewalk. Now, here she was, in our own dining room, setting a place for herself alongside our own at the round oak table.

Muriel went to the buffet, pulling the odor away from me, the odor of that night, and I came back into the present.

Alex says it's a librarian's nature to withhold advice or instructions, but expect them nevertheless to be followed; but this intrusion was too ominous for my silence. In the middle of dinner I spoke: "We know who you are."

"What?" she asked in a feathery way, but closer to that of a fowl than a member of the heavenly host.

"We took your lunch box when we were kids. We didn't know any better. We'll make it up to you if you leave; go away, without harming us."

She had made such a fuss over the Beaujolais, I suppose, because she had put something in it to knock me out. I awoke in the middle of the night. I don't remember anything between my assertion at the table and my waking. I had to get to Clay, to warn him.

I crept upstairs to his room, opening the door with absolute stealth, as I used to do. I remembered the tactile map I used to follow in the dark when I couldn't sleep so many years ago. It was easier now; I knew he wouldn't have any projects out all over his carpet; I could make it all the way to his bed without . . .

"Hey," he said quietly, "I thought we had a pact"—he opened the covers and I slid in—"to sleep separately while we had company. Thanks for breaking it; I just lie here and think about you, Muriel," he whispered, confusing our names in his sleepiness. He pulled me to him, naked, more flesh, muscle, and hair than the night of the lightning, but precisely the same temperature and odor. Suddenly, he pushed me away and bunched the brown bachelor sheet and quilt Mom had pieced between us. I couldn't see in the dark, but I could recall the details even better in my mind than I would be able to see them in ordinary light. "Evelyn, please go back to your room. Now." He said it sadly; I knew he didn't want me to.

He sat up, turning on his lamp, put the pillow modestly across his lap. I didn't move. "Evelyn, go back to your room. I'll keep the light on for you until you get downstairs."

"I just want to talk."

"Me too. Let's talk in the morning."

Why was he speaking so distantly? Then I looked up and saw her in the doorway, like a jagged line of light coming out of the darkness.

Somehow, I've forgotten what happened next, until the next morning. Muriel, in a blue eyelet dress, informed me that Clay had gone off to quarrel on the long-distance phone with a film distributor; she sat me before an absurd breakfast of berries, milk, and an egg perched in a pedestal. I was being humored. I demanded that she take it all away. "I like to see the table bare." She withdrew the food; she folded the cloth, sliding it back into a drawer. I knew she'd report me to Clay, but I couldn't take the risk of her drugging me—or of winning me over by not drugging me. My senses had to remain sharp.

I felt her presence go out of the house and at last I relaxed. My bare feet found the curved eagle claw they used to rest on when I had lived in the house and sat at the table. My elbows propped my face up from the reflected one on the polished surface; I felt my bones reinstate my childhood angles at the table. I looked absently at the space in the curtains until stunningly Muriel came into view.

She pulled a white lilac from the gnarled little tree. My stomach turned as I watched Muriel inhale the fragrance with great gasps of breath.

Abruptly Muriel's eyes snapped to focus on something in the air beyond the house; she poised in fascination, her mouth still bent and loose, fondling the lilac, her tongue finding each tiny four-sided blossom. She bit them off one by one, eating them, as simply as a gawking child at a county fair with a cotton candy, but somehow more disturbing, like a hunted animal pulling life from its victim, eye to the horizon.

I saw then the object of Muriel's gaze swoop into view and land in the lilacs. Then another. Grosbeaks. Their dazzling yellow emphasized by black-rimmed wings made the lilacs, the sky, the masquerading woman fade like a photograph. The light shifted; a dozen grosbeaks, like a single being, filtered into the lilac tree. Muriel dropped her mutilated lilac spray, raised her arms to the birds and they scattered, birds and shadows of birds. One of them seemed to depart right through Muriel's shoulder, another disappeared into her hip.

I found myself sobbing so hard I couldn't stop, or breathe, or talk, when Clay found me, still in place at the table.

He carried me into the next room, to the old couch; I've never been able to say whether it was once green or once brown, its three cushions in this house before we were born. Three cushions: one for Dad who died on the couch, one for Mom who had her stroke on it, one for me—the angel come to torture me. Clay tried to arrange my robe around me, all the more a shroud. I choked and screamed, my throat couldn't remember how to perform the release of weeping. Muriel appeared in the archway; she and Clay looked at each other. She gave him a damp washcloth and went away.

Clay sat down on the floor, holding my hand for a while, then my head, then his own head. I didn't care to cry anymore. "Clay," I said and startled him, "she's a monster. She eats the lilacs and birds fly through her. I saw. Get rid of her. She'll do something horrible to us all."

"What is that, sister? What are you afraid of?"

"She's an angel. She'll mix us up." The weight of my logic, a burden I could not get him to share, threatened to crush the breath out of me again.

"No, Evelyn. She's not an angel. She's a woman. The angel is an old secret between you and me. Let's keep it. Okay? I wanted you to come down here and spend some time with Muriel because I'm going to marry her. Even if you don't like her and don't want me to." He said evenly, "I'm going to live with her the rest of my life. I love her. And the feeling is so strange to me. I could only compare it to a boy's encounter with an angel—with a mystery."

"The angel's between us."

"I wanted you to celebrate this with us," he said mildly, as he couldn't match my intensity.

"It's not what God intends."

"Evvy, God is not one of your specialties; you've never had an interest before."

"It's like mating with an ostrich or a goose—only worse. It mixes up the universe. People can't live with angels."

"There's no such thing as an angel! This is some sort of old joke from when we were kids."

"Don't try that now. You think I don't remember what she looked like that first time? Don't you think I see?"

"But that's the amusing coincidence, Evelyn. And, to me, it's a touching coincidence. Muriel looks something like the woman I made up when I was a little boy."

"I saw her too! You never realize I saw her too!"

Muriel came in with a tablet perched on her open palm, a glass of water in her other hand. I knew they had been drugging me. To their surprise, I took it willingly. They didn't know I kept it under my tongue and spit it out under my pillow when they put me back in my bed.

They didn't realize I stood in the dining room and listened to them in the kitchen.

"She seems to feel that she's discovered you're an angel," said Clay.

"By what evidence?"

"She saw you eating a flower and a bird pass through you."

"Shadows," Muriel corrected softly.

"Yes, of course, only a shadow."

"Oh, but she's right. I mean her evidence is proper even if her conclusion might be wrong. Do you remember that old legend?"

"What? If it wasn't put on the silver screen, I don't remember it."

"Some old story that tells of a careless angel in flight"— Muriel tipped back her porcelain face as she spoke, and no one saw me at the door listening—"who permitted a sparrow to fly through its knee. The sparrow, being merely a sparrow, noticed nothing. The angel found it exhilarating. The next thing God knew, the angel was stationed every evening within the flight pattern of a flock of starlings coming in to roost. They would nearly blacken the sky, looking almost like a billowing cloth; they'd pierce right through the angel, and the angel would sing out. The starlings, unpleasant even as birds go, never felt the body of an angel. God tolerated this. But then one day, the angel saw a beautiful human being. You know, I can't remember whether in the story the angel was male and the human being was a girl, or the angel was female and the person was a boy. Anyway, what difference does it make? The angel fell in love. I guess you'd call it. Or just fell. He allowed the tip of his wing to brush through a lock of her hair. And not only did the angel feel it, so did the girl. The next thing you know, it was..."

"Full frontal angel," chuckled Clay.

"Well, yes, but I remember the story from years ago; it really was very sweetly told. God punished the angel by sending him to live as a mortal; but the angel, so much in love, didn't seem to mind—and after a while, didn't even recall having been an angel."

"Except that people noticed he really got off on bird-watching." He grinned and pulled her into his arms.

"No." She laughed after they kissed. "The story ends by saying that God has to wait for the angel to remember its true nature so that the universe can get on with its harmony or destiny or something. Every time angels love humans, the universal order is disrupted, and God, devoted as he is to free will, has to wait it out."

"That's no story." I could hardly hear Clay; he was talking into her neck and hair. "Stories end happily-ever-after. Or else, the girl finds out he's really an angel and it's a tragedy."

"Why would it be a tragedy?"

"For God," he said; his hand was under her dress. I could see her long fingers grasp that foolish brass belt-buckle Clay wears. I ran to my room and found the drug under my pillow and swallowed it down without water. I needed to sleep; then I would think.

I must have slept through to nearly dawn. Outside my window, I could see Muriel, next to our woods. She was bending over, digging a hole. Her robe twisted in the wind, resembling the folded garments of the annunciation angel, or starlings gathering at her thighs.

She had beautifully shaped legs; I could see even at that distance. Had she taken on the form just to snare Clay, or was it heavenly shaping to please God? In spite of myself I saw a grotesque version of Dante's great rose done up with old Hollywood musical legs and smiles. (*The Divine Comedy* is filed under PQ 4302. No one checks it out.) I despaired; the celestial and the celluloid had merged, not in their relationship, but in my own wadded memories.

I nevertheless pulled myself from depression's abyss by the force of my curiosity. What was Muriel burying out there by my trees?"

I wouldn't let her get away with it. I stepped through the open window, onto the porch, just as I used to do, to catch these premorning winds that were so mysterious in Stoddard Hills, before the sun burned away everything not attentive to itself. I was barefoot and silent, just as I used to meet Clay, secretly under the trees, denying our parents' concern that we sleep. I rejoiced in the exceptional wakefulness that has been with me all of my life. Alex calls it insomnia, but he's wrong. It's wakefulness. Clay has it too, pure siblings that we are.

Muriel didn't hear me coming up behind her. Whatever she was burying required a large vault, and it opened as big a gap in my mind.

Then I saw, barely discernible in the light just before sunrise, one fanned against the tree trunk, the other spread on the earth. Her wings. They looked like a helpless creature killed rather than a part of herself severed.

What sort of being was she who could dispose of her own wings—just so she'd be here forever with Clay? "But Clay will die and then what will you do?"

She whirled around and gazed at me. I realized I must have spoken out loud.

"You can't," I screamed. "You've got to keep the wings so you can get back. You've got to get back. You don't belong here."

She cast her wings into the pit.

I fell on the ground and reached for them. To touch them sent threads of energy through my hands.

Somehow Alex was there; they must have called him to come down. (I hope he remembered the note I left him, to have the muffler checked on his car.)

Clay was making up lies to him, "On top of everything, old Aggie's goose, Cookie, died yesterday. Aggie asked Muriel to bury it, claiming Muriel understood the goose better than the rest of us." Which one of them was touching me, pulling at me? I couldn't tell. "Muriel decided," he went on like a bad voice-over, "since we'd all had such a bad time, she'd just take care of it quietly, by herself, and especially so Evelyn wouldn't see ..."

"I see," I told him, told them, "I see. Don't think I can't see what's going on."

I could see that the sun had finally popped up like a full bladder of paint, looking as if it were in danger of being pierced by all the cacophonous, agitated birds. The yellow heat could run out all over us.

The birds are so noisy; we should have made a list of all the kinds of birds around here.

Ice Cream Birth

*L*AUGHING AND MURMURING, THEY *rowed across the night lake, their flashlights like lonely light-ning bugs over the water. Donna crawled into the army mummy bag out on the sun porch, watching until her eyes ached, hearing them hoot and complain until she slept. She woke when they came back at dawn with a bag full of frogs. She hopped to meet them, stumbling inside the sleeping bag, saying, "I'm a mummy! I'm a mummy!" Warren stepped on the tail of the bag and her dad pulled her out of it. They were still acting like old army buddies, as close as they were in the war. "Now you're just a kid," Bill said as he threw her in the air and Warren caught her. They laughed all morning, smearing their undershirts as they cut the frogs in half. The front halves of the frogs tried to walk away, spilling their entrails behind them; the back legs jerked, even when they were turned in the hot butter. And her dad and Warren laughed as they ate them because they said the little bastards tried to keep walking.*

It was right after he came back from Korea, Donna

thinks, and if she were not flying toward Korea those dissipated memories would not be converging. How could the fates call her name from obscure Korea and unwelcome memory?

Donna flies into ever-unfolding darkness, over water like a long spell of grief infesting the passengers with melancholy. Merchants, military, teachers, and ecclesiastics walk the aisles in their socks, amnesiacs over the clouds.

"Have you been to Korea before?" The bald man she had ignored over the vast Pacific leans toward her.

"No." She recalls the old letters from Korea.

Mysterious deliveries, she could read few of the words that her mother clung to. Her father boldly printed FREE *on the envelopes where everyone else had to lick three-cent stamps. She had admired his cavalier's pen; it was, she understood, what he was fighting for, freedom to spurn the stamp tyrants who demanded passage on private correspondence.*

"Your sweetheart over here with Uncle Sam?"

"No. I'm . . ." Donna doesn't know how to explain that Claudia's too sick to travel, too sick to take care of her child, too stubborn to leave her husband again; that she is traveling thousands of miles to retrieve a five-year-old niece she's never met, Claudia's child for merely a year; that in one letter stuffed with pictures, Claudia had announced the adoption, in the next she had admitted her own rapid cancer.

"Sorry." The man examines her face. "I'll mind my own business and good luck to you. Except, dear, have your story straight or they'll hold you up in Seoul."

When the flight attendant distributes the entry forms, Donna's pen hesitates. Bill, too, had sent photographs from Korea. *"He's so thin," her mother said. "He has a mustache," Donna said. The snapshots didn't seem to resemble anyone that either of them knew. He had labeled them on the back, his ballpoint etching the paper. Her mother read them to her. "Me and Warren. This guy's name is Fingers. Warren, Jim, Me, Pampalone, Potts, Stanton. Some kids. Warren took this of me. This is a cave full of dead gooks."* Donna stared into the glossy black, trying to glimpse the gooks. *"What're gooks?"* *"I don't know why he sent that,"* her mother had answered.

The man's shiny head leans near again. "I know you're not feeling well. But, dear, when I said have your story straight, I should have said simple. The fewer words, the fewer snags. Best to put down tourism. Don't explain to those whose job is mistrust."

"My sister's very ill. She's unable to care for Tess. Her husband's always going on maneuvers or something."

"Yes, I see. That's tourism. Write tourism. How old is Tess?"

"Almost five." It was Donna's age when her dad followed his letters across the ocean and back into their house.

"Lucky you, lucky sister to have you to help her get well. You have other children?"

"No, I'm not married. And Steve, the man I live with, is not sure he wants to take on a child. And neither am I." She is ashamed of her loose tongue.

"You won't be traveling alone?"

"Yes. Well, no. With Tess."

"The little girl?"

"Yes."

"We had no children, my wife and I. Now, you're going to think you met a crazy man, but sitting here while you cried and slept all night, I just got a feeling for you. Don't get me wrong. I can see you feel like I did before Norma passed away. You know, her wedding ring kept sliding off. She just wasted away. Then she says, when I picked it up off the sheet, 'Give that ring to our daughter.' I say, 'What, hon?' She says, 'Give my ring to our girl.' Those were her last words and I put it here on my little finger. Here it's been for two years. I've been trying to figure what she wanted me to do with it. I saw your hand last night when you fell asleep. I just knew Norma wanted you to have it."

"Please..."

"I'm not going to bother you. I'm not even going to ask your name. But a wedding ring helps a woman traveling alone." He grabs her hand and sticks the wide, gold ring on her finger. "And it just fits!"

She struggles to remove the ring. He holds her hand in his as though it were a trapped, live animal. People turn to watch. Donna stops and sits speechless.

"Here's my card. Call me anytime, day or night. My answering service will tell you where to reach me. I'll expect to hear from you."

Donna stands in line at Kimpo Airport examining noses, gait, weight of hair, turn of an arm, looking for puzzle pieces that would fit her own body, hidden siblings on the reverse side of the world. Between her own age and Claudia's, she thinks; going to her own failing sister, she seeks kindred blood concealed in the marketplaces—*how many hidden in this picture? She helped little Claudia find the mouse in the cloud, the shoe in the tree trunk, the president in the water.* She looks for the unintentional brother or sister her father might have left in Korea.

"Sissy. Got a kiss for me?"

Donna turns her face and her brother-in-law presses his thin mustache, like a crowd of insects on a line of honey, against her cheek. "Now," he clamps her in his arm, "I'm gonna tell you something, and you're not going to make a scene. These little bureaucrats jump on any disturbance. The only reason they let anyone through is because they love stamping things."

"They didn't trouble me at all. They're nice." Donna looks into Roger's hazel eyes reflecting the color of his uniform and expects him to say Claudia is down, worse.

"Claudia passed on. Four days ago. We cremated her so everything's okay," he says inexplicably. Donna tries to pull away from him, the paranoia, the obituary; he folds her into his name tag, ribbons, and bars, hissing in her face, "Don't carry on."

"Where's Tess?"

"Right over here with Sung Yi. I've hired him to help out. Your flights back to the States couldn't be changed. So, he'll be taking you down to Kyong Ju, over to Tokyo and Kyoto, back here. He'll show you all the culture. By then I'll have all Tess's stuff packed up, papers ready, and you'll be off."

"Did you think of discussing my travel plans with me?"

"Don't try to fuck things up. I've done the best I can. I don't want Tess sitting around the house. She's spooked. So, be a tourist, take her along and get to know her. Sung Yi speaks Japanese besides American."

"English."

"Yeah. And Korean, of course. So you won't get in any trouble. Besides, Tess likes him." Tess, in the arms of the grinning Sung Yi, is the vision of what Claudia had loved. Cream had been poured into her complexion, a little spring to her hair. Donna notices her dimpled hand.

"Will there be a problem for her to leave the country?" Donna's sudden desire for her must be, she thinks, an exchange for her routed grief.

"Don't worry, Sissy, she's a one hundred percent Americano. No one can stop her. Call her Tess. None of those kim-chi rotten cabbage names for my kid," he says. "And, don't ever let anybody think it's Teresa. It's Tesla. If I didn't finish my engineering degree, she can finish hers."

"I want to visit Claudia's. . ." She could not say grave, and could not ask why a memorial service was not arranged so she could be present.

"Uh, when you come back from Tokyo everything will be arranged."

She would carry back a child, not for a few months, but. . . *"for keeps."* She hears Claudia's childhood voice and remembers her dad saying, *"They buried their good dishes.*

They didn't want the Americans to find them." "Were they afraid you'd want them for keeps?" Claudia had asked. In all those years the men rarely spoke of the world they had glimpsed, nor of combat, nor of death; but they carried the war home, like leeches, behind their necks, under their bellies and thighs. They came home, and the war survived, in dormant memory. In the first few years, Bill would cross his leg and a remnant sock, the color of official aggression, would burst out like a fragment of a rousing, surly song. One time Bill and Warren drank and sang, "We Are Truman's Little Lambs," though her mother commented, "Well, now we've got Eisenhower." Donna sang it to baby Claudia. "Don't sing that," Bill had said, "that's no song for a little girl." "Because now we've got Eisenhower?" Donna asked.

In Seoul, everyone carries a folded cotton handkerchief, patting forehead and neck, keeping a crisp manner, defying the liquid air. Donna wipes at her face with the back of her hand. No one told her to bring a hanky. Among the gifts Bill brought home were two boxes of delicate embroidered hankies. Donna's mother had said, "Aren't they pretty." She put them in a drawer and never unfolded them. After the Korean War, women no longer carried lace hankies; they kept five-cent handy packs of kleenexes in their purses. Donna can't find a tissue to mop her neck or brow; having spent them on Claudia's illness, she has none to spend on death or weather. The boxes of hankies were still there after both parents were dead; Donna and Claudia packed them up with almost everything else for the Sisters of Mercy. "Mom told me once," Claudia had whispered, "that he was changed by the war. The 'police action.' No one cared then. No protesters. And women didn't complain. Didn't have expectations, like now, she said." "What else did she say?" asked Donna, a little jealous. "That he was real sweet before. That he came back 'rougher.' And after that he 'talked so rough, nothing seemed to mean too much to him,' and that 'everything seemed temporary. Even people.' That's all she'd say; she was always *loyal." Donna said, "You're too young to remember when I found his letters to her. They caught me reading them and Dad made her burn them." "Oh, Sissy, why? What did they say?" "Mostly 'Dearest Darling' stuff. She was sorry to lose them, you could tell. She just laughed, though, and said he didn't want any clues around to his soft heart." "Viet Nam changed things." "For everybody except you, Claudia." "You can't equate Roger with the military." "You're just like Mom. Blindly loyal." "Let's not fight. You'll learn to love Roger. You're my whole family now," she hugged Donna, "and I'm going to be good to you, 'cause you might need me someday." Claudia dug down in the big box and retrieved the embroidered hankies, pressing them on Donna with an apologetic, shy laugh.*

Finding the hotel, Roger takes them to their room. "Sung Yi has orders to take care of you and my baby. I'll meet you back here the twenty-fifth. Sorry, I've got duty."

She looks at the way he cups his hand around Tess's head. "You're her blood father, aren't you?"

"I conquered a little Korea. Don't know a man who doesn't. No one ever knocked any sense into you about men; you're high and mighty just because you're ignorant."

"This is your biological child. Did Claudia know?"

"She wasn't like you; she didn't beat people over the head with their own lives."

"What do you know about Tess's birth mother?" Donna asks. Sung Yi unpacks her clothes.

Roger breaks into a smile, a pink slit under his tan mustache. "Well, Miss Priss, this is even funnier. I never told Claudia, by the way. Her mom is named Su Lin, born in 1951. Sorry to cheat you out of your Korean orphan, so you can brag back home, but Su Lin was born in 1951. Get it? You only got yourself a one-quarter slant."

"That's your daughter."

"She's my baby. I don't care if she's got three eyes,

and all of 'em like grains of rice. It's you I despise, Sissy."

"Why?"

"Because you look like Claudia, only you're not sweet, and you keep pretending you don't want me in your pants. You're no different from Claudia, so you see, Sissy, I know better. I know what you want."

"Maybe it's grief and impotence that make you brutal."

"What do you mean, impotence?"

"Don't be stupid, Roger. I mean the 38th Parallel. I mean Korea and politics."

"You don't know shit about politics." He kisses and tickles the silent Tess, and leaves.

Donna gathers Tess onto her lap. The child perches stiffly. "Would you like to come to America with me? You will go to school there; we'll have a puppy; when I come home from work, we'll cook together; we'll look at pictures, draw, and swim. We'll read books you choose. Please come with me."

"I am coming to America. My dad already told me."

"It's scary now. But you'll like it very much."

"My mom's not there."

"No. Did your dad talk to you about Mom?"

She nods and runs toward the window. When Donna starts to speak, Tess covers her ears with her hands. Donna sits beside her, looking out the window at the mountain. "It's beautiful, isn't it? Namsan."

Tess says nothing.

"And the city looks beautiful beneath it?"

"It's all shacked down," Tess mutters.

"Those are interesting streets, don't you think? Over there is where we saw the children playing yut."

"Turn on terebi."

Sung Yi turns it on. "You rest now. Dinner will come to room. I come back in morning."

"Sung Yi, I appreciate your attention, but we'll be fine by ourselves."

"No. Sorry. I owe Captain big debt. He say this how I

got to pay up. See you early in morning." Tess hurries to hug him as he leaves.

The U.S. Forces channel punctuates old movies with one-minute dramas about the old gang of losers at home who admire the best of the bunch, the hero who signed up with Uncle Sam. Innocuous community bulletins—free aerobics, picnics, babysitting exchanges—are voiced over images of menacing battleships and swarming soldiers. "Shall we turn it off?"

Tess glares at her.

"Are you ready for a bath?"

"Okay," she says, but Donna knows that beneath Tess's bland voice, as on the television, is a visceral, combative image.

Donna's tears fall as she soaps and rinses Tess, beautiful, silent as the dolls she replicates. And, Donna thinks, Claudia ransomed her child by remaining mute, pretending ignorance of the illicit relationship between the birth parents. And Claudia, through multiple misconceptions, was blessed with mothering. Donna wraps one towel as a sarong, one as a turban, "Look how pretty you are."

"You are not my mom," Tess says, but permits herself to be dried, combed, and tucked into instant sleep. Donna wakes over and over through the night, not just to check the child, nor to prod her distending grief, but to resist the penetrating, aggressive odor of Seoul.

The military swarms the streets with the first light, the shopkeepers follow. The department store clerks poise for the national anthem, then white-gloved like Disney's mice, they stand alert over their little specialized territories.

Tess stealthily touches the silk of the elevator hostess; embroidered cranes run the green flutter of the gown. "Let's get Tess a traditional dress," Donna says.

"Do this now?" Sung Yi asks.

"Yes."

He leads her to the labyrinth of tourist shops that spread

from under the hotel and guides her to a tiny shop. Sung Yi speaks Korean and the shopkeepers laugh expansively, touching Donna's skin and hair. Tess is handed a small folded garment, brilliant pink, stamped with gold designs.

"I want an authentic dress, not for tourists," Donna says helplessly.

"This genuine," Sung Yi says firmly, stepping out of the shop.

"Good. Cheap price." The saleswomen chatter around her like birds, unfolding another dress, "This for big girl," and they begin to try it on her. As Donna protests, she catches a glimmer of interest in Tess's eyes. "When you wear this dress, don't wear bra. Korean women never wore these," says the bold shopkeeper. Sung Yi pokes his head back in and they all laugh again, as the asymmetrical bow is tied with the good luck beaded cord.

Despite their teasing, Donna gushes, "The Korean traditional dress is the most beautiful design in the world."

"This is chima. This is chogori. Skirt and top. Korea invaded many times by soldiers. The women wear these dresses to hide they expecting child, so enemy not know, not harm."

Under which bell is the pea? Donna thinks; all women must appear pregnant to hide those who are. *Those goddamn do-gooders back in the States put up a racket 'cause we had to strip those Korean women at the checkpoints. They said we were 'disrobing innocent women.' That we were 'molesting them.' Hell, they were carryin' grenades and ammunition in those goddamn bloomers. What were we supposed to do?"*

"Pretty," says Tess, startling and pleasing Donna.

"I'll get this too, so she'll have it when she's grown up." We'll never be back, she thinks; I'll have Tess forever, but Korea will recede again into the pit of forgetting. Tess hangs on to her bright dress, so only Donna's dress and tassle are wrapped like a gift. *"Every shop has a charming wrap, and every sale is completed as a kind of celebration, confusing commerce and presents,"* Claudia had written her, *"even a pair of socks from Eastgate—from a woman whose stall is the size of our closet in the old house, and whose entire inventory is socks. She forgives me, I feel, all that is grotesque in my life and hers; as she wraps the socks, she gives them to me so I am not guilty of purchase. And she returns, to herself and to me, all our dignity."*

After that, Claudia hardly mentioned Korea. Her letters illuminated smaller and smaller spaces, as she seemed to take on the talent for miniaturization from her hosts. Until the letter came which said, *"I am so exhausted with this thing, it weighs on my chest at night, leaving no room for breath or sleep. Then, I conceived the idea of you coming here to get Tess, taking her home. And I could feel her in your arms, I could see her in your lap, I could hear her chiming in on your stories of the great artists, I could see you both playing with those fancy pencils you bring home from work, and it all came into me like a cool light. Please, Sissy, Tess is a beautiful child. I know Steve will resist—until he meets her. You may not think you are ready for this, she may not even need you. But, I must be released from this bed. Come. Take her while I wrestle with these sweaty demons. Thinking you are on your way, I can sleep."*

"Sung Yi, how did you meet Roger?" she asks in the Land of the Morning Calm and Rising Suspicions.

"I work for many Americans. They cannot learn Korean. Americans not very smart, Don-na." He laughs.

"What sort of business is Roger involved in?"

"Good ones. Make money. Captain says, 'Plenty fish.' "

"Yes, but . . ."

"You ask Captain."

Bill and Warren came back with a catch of fish after two days' pursuit of a remote rumor of plenty. "There were so many fish," *Warren crowed,* "they shoved each other out of the way to hang themselves on the hook." "I don't want

*to eat those damn things. Get rid of them," Bill said. "What?
You didn't say anything before." "Look, they were so over-
crowded, there wasn't enough to eat; their bodies never caught
up with their heads. Those bastards put me in mind of Korea.
That's what the gooks looked like."* Donna admires the con-
tours of Sung Yi's big golden face and heavy rich hair, dis-
proportionate by her customed Western eye, with his slen-
derness. "Is the beautiful dependent more upon custom
than surprise?" she asks aloud. Sung Yi looks bewildered.

"Everything's so small it breaks when the GIs touch it,"
a letter said. *"We have to use what we can so we don't freeze
to death, so we take their little houses. They're not much.
The people are gone anyway. They dig tunnels under their
floors so smoke goes through the tunnels to warm the dirt
floor. But GIs build the fires too hot—wanting what's home.
The Koreans don't wear shoes in the house, and combat
boots on those floors make the tunnels collapse and the little
houses only last a few days now. But that's all we need and
then we're gone. Sometimes sooner. Still, you'd think those
tunnels under the floor are a pretty good idea."*

"I want to see the real market," Donna demands.

Sung Yi presses his lips together, his black eyes look
past her.

He takes them to the turmoil of Namdaemoon; Donna
and Tess stand gazing in opposite directions until a handcart
rams Donna's hip. She pulls Tess from its path, and then
sees its driver, a man like a seal. Pulling himself along on
his belly, a sandal on one hand, an old black shoe on the
other, trailing a canvas bag holding whatever tatters of legs
and trunk, he propels his cart with his shoulder. She had
wondered whom her father might have killed, even the
progeny he might have sired, about the orphans he might
have left behind from love or death, but she had never
considered whom he might have maimed. If he did not
come back whole, he must have left wounds too.

A chorus of pigs' heads gaze from their tiered rack
toward a painted cock and ginseng, over tubs of slender

eels, bins of shoes, piles of contorted metal, and the man like a seal, pressing his cart through the crowd. Is this the place, Donna asks herself, where her father damaged his own sweet, soft heart? *A deaf man once came into their yard, handing Bill a business card which explained and begged. Donna watched her dad keep his head down, growl quietly, "Get the hell out of here," and the man had fled. "See," he had said to her, "the son-of-a-bitch wasn't deaf at all." Later, they went inside and found Skippy scattering the garbage all over the house again. Bill took his gun and the dog to the woods and came back with the gun. "See. That dog wasn't no good anymore. Back home, we always shot a dog once it wasn't no good to nobody."*

The high-spirited flirtations everywhere she goes begin to wear on Donna, making her feel odd and pink and lonely.

"See, everyone watches; everyone envies me because I'm with you," confides Sung Yi.

"Tess, darling," Donna says, picking her up, ignoring him, "you are doing important work on earth. You are scrambling genes."

"What?" frowns Sung Yi.

"Changing minds."

"Your English is harder to know than others."

Tess stares at a gigantic floating ginseng root in a jar that could accommodate Tess herself. The root promises exceptional, grotesque, sexual energy. "What do you think, Tess?" Tess keeps quiet. "What's this about? All these ginseng shops? Though I do like the ways babies are born in this country: from gourds, from eggs, from a golden box."

"Back home evertime we went squirrel huntin', we'd dig ginseng and stick them in our pockets. We laid 'em out on a hot windowsill to dry them out. When we'd get a coffee sack full, we'd sell it. Those crazy bastards over there thought it would make them young again. Made me the best money a kid ever saw during the Depression." "What'd you buy?" "Shotgun shells and a picture show."

•

The next day, Sung Yi packs them up and drives them to Kyong Ju. "Five hours maybe. Don't cry all the way," he says as Donna broods.

"What are all the flowers along the road?"

"Korea's national flower," he announces.

"What are they called?"

"Forget." Seeing her irritation, he provides substitute information, "See this highway? This really only four-lane highway. Why you think this look like six-lane highway?"

Donna has no idea what his riddle is aiming at.

"When war starts, this is where the planes land." He laughs and looks at her. "Rose of Sharon. Flower is called Rose of Sharon," he glowers.

She remembers her dad's history of the war in one of his letters. *The goddamn Marines were cut off at Chosin Reservoir. So of course the Army was sent in to get them out. We did. The Chinese just kept coming in those little padded suits. They got them wet. So when night came and it got so cold, the Chinks froze to death. But they got plenty more Chinese, they don't care. It's always either too hot or too cold here. I don't know what anybody wants with it. The old men look good in their stovepipe hats. Make them out of varnished horsehair. Our water tank froze up. We had to build a fire underneath the truck trailer to thaw it.*

Donna looks out the window, "Rice paddies. I've never seen them before. Christ, how can Roger expect me to endure this? How can he expect Tess to hold up under all this pointless travel?"

"Captain. He licks skin of watermelon."

"What?"

"Only know outside."

"Superficial. So, that little folk painting we got for Steve, of the rats eating seeds from a watermelon they've broken into. They're okay, those rats. That's why it looks oddly happy, all vines and butterflies?"

"Is happy."

"Subak," chirps Tess from her nest in the backseat.

"What is she saying?"

"Watermelon," he laughs. "Maybe Subok. Long life and happy life."

"How much Korean does she speak?"

"Captain says I should not speak Korean to Tess. Only English."

They stop to see the mounds, burial sites of kings. They go down in one great sod belly and Donna stands before the sifted remains. Denied her sister's gruesome death, but she is forced by that death to gaze upon others, turned by time to beauty and meaning. Her sister's gone, but the invisible king is etched into his stately rest.

They walk up a winding, forested road toward the Sok-kuram, the great tranquil Buddha in his artificial cave. Sung Yi entertains Tess with the mottled frogs which imitate the appearance of the mossy rocks and urges her to drink and wash with the purifying waters; Donna snaps her mind shut over her notions of hygiene. Yet, before the gigantic stone Sakyamuni, she feels its limitless compassion touch the limits of her shadowed consciousness.

"This one here," Sung Yi indicates one of the surrounding figures. "She is Konnan. She will not forget. Mercy."

"I am interested in the art. Not the religion," Donna says spitefully.

"Yes. I know. Captain tell me what you like to see. You would fit," he says to Tess, "in the Buddha's mouth."

"Big," says Tess.

"Good," says Sung Yi. "He take care," he whispers to Tess. "Tell me difference, Don-na. Art. Religion."

"Ask Roger."

"Captain say all bullshit."

Another time, she could be awed by Silla crowns, all Tao jade and spangled gold; on another occasion, she'd feel something for the headless granite figures. But now she feels like a drifting shade. An elegant Matraiya Buddha, golden, serene, evokes Warren's wife with the delicate hands. *Mioko sometimes visited with Donna alone in her room. Mioko held baby Claudia on her lap and arranged her wisps of hair. Mioko made her mother feel calm. Donna told her dad Mioko was the most beautiful woman in the world.* "Yeah. Well, it's not right. I wouldn't marry Mioko if she had a gold butt." "Why?" *exclaimed Donna.* "You know why. She's a Jap." *Donna thought perhaps Mioko did have a gold butt.* Looking at the rounded, gleaming Buddhas, she sees her childhood mirage of a naked Mioko. Even then, Donna smiles, she had surmised no one would have claimed a solid, gold-butted woman for a wife, a perfection flawed for elementary functions.

"You know this bell," says Sung Yi, playing the tour guide, "very old, this bronze bell. They cast it and it will not ring. They have to find woman, woman so poor, when everyone give something for bell, she tell the monk, 'I only have baby. I give it.' When baby born, they forget. Then King find out why bell can't ring. Tell Monk, get the baby. Monk goes to woman and says give your little baby, she make bell ring, good for many people. Good life for baby. They melt bell, throw baby in; bell come out round, smooth as baby. Her cry in sound of bell."

"Just stop it," Donna turns away.

"Look, angels. Very famous angels cast on bell. Very famous art." He shrugs, "I take you to hotel now."

Tess runs to an arcade game outside the lobby.

"You too small. You little girl. I show you."

"No," says Donna, "don't turn it on."

Sung Yi inserts his coins, stands poised with a large mallet chained to the game like a librarian's pencil. Martial music, the sounds of firing and of men shouting, burst from the tinny speaker, as nearly life-size rubber heads of evil-looking North Koreans pop erratically from their foxhole slots and Sung Yi gleefully beats them back into the ground.

"Stop. Please. It's hideous," says Donna. Tess giggles and claps her hands. Sung Yi picks her up, she puts her arms around him.

"You want to be her momma. You should be soft."

Donna's eyes spill with tears, "Soft. Soft. You bash heads, you club your brother, and you dare to tell me..."

"It just fun game. You don't have fun. Tess lonely for momma."

"You think I'm not lonely? Now my whole family's dead, and I'm supposed to change my life to invent a family out of the remains of the betrayals and carelessness of warfare?"

Sung Yi looks at her. "Yes. Don-na. I see you miss your sister. I will take Tess to walk across bridge to see frogs jump in pond. You will miss Tess while we are gone. Then," he smiles, "then we have dinner, as Captain say."

"Sung Yi, I don't know why Roger hired you; I'm an adult, capable of traveling myself. Consider it simply that he was out of his mind because Claudia's life was beyond his control; I went along with his plan because I was surprised and disoriented. But I will not be patronized."

"That's ol' Fingers," Bill had pointed at the figure in the photograph. The boy looked back at her, small, glossy, black and white. "Why was his name Fingers?" " 'Cause the little shit stole anythin' that wasn't nailed down." "It wasn't his real name. Why did you take this picture?" "He was a cute little shit." "What did you do when he stole?" "One time Kelly grabbed him and pulled out his buck knife and said, 'You little bastard, you steal one more thing and I'm gonna cut off your thievin' fingers.' Poor little kid pissed his pants." "Then what happened?" Bill's laugh carried past the house, "Fingers waited 'til Kelly's back was turned and stole the knife." "What did he steal from you?" "Nothing. He knew I woulda chopped off his fingers." Donna wondered if he was telling the truth. "I'd always find him sitting in my tent. I taught him to play poker. When he made twenty bucks the first time I staked him, then Kelly wanted to cut his throat."

"Where were his parents?" "Didn't have none. Most of those kids was orphans, so they followed the GIs around." "How did they get dinner?" "They lined up every day with their little buckets and we filled them up. One little shit kept emptyin' her bucket into a big one behind the bush and runnin' back into line." "Did you yell at her?" "I winked at her. She didn't know what I was gonna do." "What'd she do with all that food?" "She fed her folks." "I thought they were orphans." "Orphans can have folks. Their village." "I wouldn't eat out of a bucket in a million years." "If you was hungry you would. It's eat hog or die."

The next day, all the way back to Seoul, Donna finds excuses not to go to Japan. "So sorry, Don-na. I keep bargain with Captain."

"It has nothing to do with me. And you should have nothing to do with him. He's not like other Americans. It makes me ashamed."

"America like rat in jar. Rat goes in jar to get rice, wife sees rat and puts top on jar. Rat can't get out."

"And the wife can't get the rice?"

He laughs, throwing his hands from the steering wheel to his head. "You right, Don-na. Rat can't get out. Wife can't get rice. Rice spoiled." He paused. "But now Korea make cars. Not just silko."

Donna had imagined charming little conversations with Tess, respectful of her birthplace. But Tess holds her tongue. So over the Sea of Japan, Donna finds herself saying, "Korea invented the folding fan" and "Korea had developed moveable print before Gutenberg in Germany." Sung Yi smiles and Tess crawls into his lap and falls asleep. Donna stares down at her smooth, blue skirt.

Tess keeps her face close to the cotton jacket she carries, clinging to the odor of Seoul.

"Those Japs," her father said, *"are clever. They can copy*

anything. There's a guy sits in the road with some neckties. He'll paint your picture right on the necktie and it'll look just like you." Clever as it was, her father said, *"I didn't give a yen to hang my face from my neck,"* to duplicate his features between his heart and his belly. If it was as clever as he claimed, shouldn't he have lingered there and had his instant portrait? Would he have been disturbed to see a slight almond painted to his eye? Shouldn't he have lingered on earth, to see Japanese technological innovation? Europe enhanced her porcelain, Vincent painted a slant to his eyes, middle America learned to stir-fry and sleep close to the floor; but Bill, who always remembered he was from Tennessee, tried to keep himself pure from Oriental notions.

The restaurants serve imitations of the plastic models of the selections in their windows, the three-dimensional menus more beautiful, more important than the copies made by mere edible foods. "Oriental platonism?" Donna asks. "What we want, we get. What we conceptualize, is born. What we fear, comes home."

"You always look at food in windows. Then you say you not hungry," Sung Yi complains. "Baby tired."

Bill had brought Donna a pair of smooth wooden dolls, with little round heads. A twist—he had to do it for her the first hundred times—and they opened, revealing smaller versions of themselves. And the smaller opened again, and again, the miraculous births multiplied. A sensible birthing, harmonious impregnations, male and female. If not, at least, the final critique of the virgin birth, they were the innuendo of infinity. In those smooth, joined wombs, those lacquered humanoid rooms, were descending orders of creative perfection: each doll at once parent and child, artist and object, portraying humanity's perfect dilemmas. "Why don't the littlest ones open?" "Then there'd be littler ones and you'd want them opened up, too." "Well, maybe just these, just once more." "Some are just not ready for babies." Her father smiled.

As Sung Yi swings Tess to his shoulders, Donna observes

three Japanese businessmen studying a restaurant window display with an American, the squat, shiny man from the plane. She quickly stuffs her hand in her pocket, noticing at the same time, as the American points toward his selection, a wide, gold band flashing on his pinky. "Quick," says Donna, pulling Sung Yi's shirt. She ducks into a seal shop.

"What you want here?"

"Oh, something with Tess's name or initial."

"Yes. Okay. Who was that American? You fear him?"

"No."

"You are CIA?" he kids her.

She removes the bald man's ring and puts it on Sung Yi's little finger.

"We married now?" He looks over his shoulder, responds to the shopkeeper in Japanese, and shepherds Donna and Tess out the door.

"What were you saying?"

"He did not like us so much."

"The Japanese hate Koreans and Americans," she sighs.

"They like Americans."

"No. They're just polite."

"They want to be like you."

"Yes. But they don't like us. They only import and imitate our junk."

Sung Yi laughs; "You want them copy your ancient culture? Okay, I sorry. We married now?"

"No. Stop it."

"Who was that man?"

"He gave me the ring. On the plane. I don't know him."

"Strange American customs. Tell Japanese. They soon give rings to strangers."

"I don't want to be here. I can't appreciate Japan with you. Or with my heavy heart."

"Sure, Don-na, I show you. Japan beautiful and you love. Here beating heart is made gentle."

They drag Tess from one temple to another. Tess oblig-

ingly sits and waves her stocking feet at the Ryoanji Rock
Garden; she drops her coins in the box and rings the bell
on Mt. Hiei; she claps for the Kami and the carp; she ties
her fortune to a twig. But she looks warily, still, at Donna.
Cicadas chant their crazed sutras to the Buddha. "The author of the silent sermon, he'd have liked all these cicadas
around his temples?" Donna asks, and when Sung Yi ignores
her, she asks, "The cicadas keep their mouths shut, sing
with their bellies, right?"

"Yes," and he catches one for Tess. She puts her hands
behind her back; Sung Yi places the cicada respectfully in
the branch of a tree. Tess points at the crackling insect.

Pilgrimage, Donna thinks, is tracing the heart's map
on the earth's face, seeking life in death's mementos, pursu-
ing secrets in magnetic areas, hurrying blood toward ashes,
bringing breath to stone, reanimating, not past epiphanies,
but recent deaths. "The tourist is a mourner," she says to
Sung Yi, looking around her, "there's nowhere to go in grief."

*"They don't like our rice," her dad told her. "Why not?"
"It's polished. We eat white rice. They keep the skin on.
Whenever we give 'em white rice, they didn't like it." "Why
didn't they polish theirs?" " 'Cause they don't eat much. If
they ate the kind of rice we do, they'd die." Even then, Donna
felt he'd let some terrible cat or skeleton loose from behind
the red, white, and blue.* Donna sees the sushis in the windows, artful color and form, devised with sticky, white rice.
*But it was her mother who was getting thinner. And when
Donna entered high school, Claudia was practicing long di-
vision at the kitchen table, and their mother made her first
trip to the hospital. By the time Donna was in college and
Claudia was flunking Geometry, their mother was dying with
determination. "Art history?" Bill had quizzed Donna after
the funeral, three years later, "What the hell kind of bullshit
is that?" Claudia pleased him more, trading English litera-
ture for devotion to strutting Roger. But before Donna moved
in with Steve, Bill placed the rifle he had used against Skippy*

in his own mouth and squeezed. "Squeeze," he said, the long-ago day he wanted to teach her to shoot, "Don't jerk." "Did you ever kill anyone in the war?" "You got your eye on that tin can? Keep your mind on it or you can't hit nothin'." Donna had sensed a flaw in the instructions—if her mind clung to the soup can, she'd blow out her own brains when she fired—just like she always knew her dad was doing all along.

"I give Tess bath; you rest," he says.

Donna lies across her bed, sticky and irritated at their soothing chatter. He puts Tess in her nightie and in her bed, turns on the television, and the little girl falls asleep before the Japanese replica of an American game show. Contestants scream and flap with goony greed all around the Pacific basin. Sung Yi sits on the edge of Donna's bed and awkwardly cools her face with a damp washcloth.

She looks at him. "You and Tess have those lovely bird eyes."

"Birds have eyes like beads."

"No. Bird bodies. The rim of your eye is framed by the horizontal outline of a bird, the beak and tail dip to meet the curve of your cheek." She lightly draws on his face.

With swift and minimal shifts of fabric, he makes efficient, shy love. Then they undress each other, curious and pleased, and shower in the tiny bathroom. He returns her to the bed, to slow, deep embraces.

Tess wakens and looks at the television excitement of teams competing to fill basins with mouthfuls of water. "Spit," says Tess and climbs into the other bed, between them.

"Do me a favor," Donna whispers. "Please don't tell Roger."

"Captain would kill me," he smiles.

"Roger wouldn't really do anything violent. He just talks like a maniac."

He looks at her darkly, then speaks to Tess in Korean.

"What did you say?"

Tess crawls out of bed and pulls Coke and rice crackers from the little refrigerator.

"I tell her to have Coke. I want to lie near her pale mother."

"Never again. This was a mistake. I wasn't thinking. Dammit, don't turn that gloom on me. I've seen enough of Korea to know you all are affectionate and funny one minute, then fierce or gloomy the next."

"You make love with my country, not me."

"No." She kisses his cheek, his hair. He doesn't respond. "Maybe. Maybe so. We meet for war, then we mate for worse."

"You feel too sorry."

"How can I grieve for my sister? I'm gathering up clichés, death mementos, for a child who doesn't want them; my father's horrific vision keeps chasing me; I keep taking off my shoes and kneeling before someone else's god; now I'm making love to a stranger. This is my grieving? This is madness."

"I'm not stranger. I pray every time to Buddha, and to Kami, too, for sister, for Don-na, for Tess."

Donna tries to amuse herself with distortions she finds of her language: "When you feel unpleasant and thirsty," "Alive Music." Through a garland of neon, she reads that a shop specializes in "Ice Cream Birth." "We try to understand one another," she says, and cries.

"They make ice cream," Sung Yi explains tenderly, as though to console her.

She's grateful to take off from Narita. "This is an island, and this is a peninsula," she shows Tess on the map. She shuts her eyes and says, "I wonder if I could be glad to leave the refined lines of Japan to return to the stormy aesthetic of Korea?"

"Your mother, we do not know her words." Sung Yi smiles, kissing Tess and gazing closely at Donna's face.

Back in Seoul, they emerge from the always clean under-
ground to the hotel side of the street. Donna sees a beggar
kneeling on a step, her forehead just above her bowl, her
child asleep on her back, his arms around her neck, his
bare feet dangling almost to the pavement. Like a grotesque
of the pietà, they look merely like death, a distortion of
misercordia. Donna wonders if the mother started begging
with an infant bound to her back. As he grew, he remained,
slowly outgrowing his emblematic ability to engender instant, casual, compassion; in another few months his feet
will touch the earth and the image will be shattered. Will
she bear another child, increase poverty's obligation? And
will the former child always sleep restlessly, no pillow, no
pallet, like his mother, the pedestal madonna? With all the
won she has left wadded in her hand, Donna stands rooted.
Tess yanks the money from her and casts the bills in the
bowl. "Gamsa hamnida," the mother mutters. "It's okay,"
says Tess and takes Donna's hand, urging her up the steps.

Roger appears the next morning, a martinet instructing
Sung Yi on the luggage.

"Did Su Lin know anything about her birth father?"

"Thought you'd never ask. For one roll in the hay, I'll
tell you."

"Tell me and stop that nonsense."

"Don't pull that crap with me. I wouldn't fuck you if
you were an oil well. I wouldn't fuck you if you were the
Empire State Building complete with Fay Wray and King
Kong. I wouldn't fuck you if you were an oyster with a pearl
necklace."

"Do you know Su Lin's mother? War games may belong
to the men, but they concede the children back to the
women."

"Her name was Nongae. You want me to give you some
sob story about women who got stuck with GIs' kids? Nope.
Sorry. Su Lin's mom's dead. Nongae. But she told Su Lin,"

and he made a little snorting sound, "her dad said he'd come back to get them; he was Bill who come from Tennessee."

"You are lying."

"You just wish. It's not painted pictures out here. It's tough. We've had three border incidents this month. You better pray you get out of here before things get tense. One of my E-5s almost got his balls blown off Friday. Whatcha got in here?" Roger asks Tess, rummaging in a large, colorful bag.

"Some little things to help her make the plane trip," Donna says.

"Junk," Roger decides.

"There were hundreds of soldiers named Bill." Donna stands over them.

"I know it. But it's something to think about, hm, Sissy?"

"See," Tess offers Roger a tiny box with a glass lid, revealing a couple of painted rice grains.

"Rice dolls, huh? What are these people?"

"Rice," she giggles.

"Here, Tess, eat the mamasan." She pushes Roger's hand away. "Well, aren't they rice? Isn't rice to eat?"

Donna asks, "What will I do when you want her back?"

"I won't take her away from you. We'll do an official adoption, if that's what you want. If you promise to let me see her."

"Of course."

"See, Sissy. I trust your word. Why can't you trust me? Okay, airhead, don't lose this." He pulls from a box a sumptuously costumed doll. Tess stares at it expectantly. "I thought you'd want Claudia's ashes, but I figured customs would raise all hell and it'd be forever before you'd clear. So a friend of mine sewed them inside this doll." He taps its body with his forefinger.

"You can't have done this grotesque thing to me."

"You only think of yourself, Donna. My wife's gone and Korea's right here. My baby's leaving for America. The world doesn't revolve around you. And I went to a lot of trouble to make it easy for you. Figured you'd be sentimental; if not, fuck it, I'll split 'er open and we'll dump the ashes in the Han." He threatens to pull the doll apart.

"Good-bye, Roger. I'll expect adoption proceedings to begin immediately. And you may see Tess whenever you're inclined."

"I can't raise her myself," his voice collapses.

"I know. You're doing what's best." But Donna wonders, is she?

He picks up Tess and her arms and legs clamp around him.

A sob bursts from his throat as he lays his sudden tears against hers. When Roger finally unfastens Tess, he reaches out to Donna, kissing her wetly, tears and tongue, all over her face and hair, welding together the lost sister and wife, the motherless child, and his own, homeless eros onto Donna's unyielding sorrows. "Sung Yi will see you get through the airport. I can't stand to see her go," he whispers, and leaves.

On the way to the airport, Sung Yi says, "This is Han River. Water for Seoul, pretty soon again. I want you learn something before you leave, Don-na."

"The River Lethe," she says with self-pity. "Wait, there is something I want to learn. Did you ever know someone named Nongae?"

"Ah, you are reading old stories. Good. Yes, Nongae was dancing girl, a legend, she holds enemy general in her arms, so they drown together."

"A real person, Sung Yi."

"Maybe."

"No, you heard what Roger said. Tess's grandmother."

"I going to miss you, Don-na."

In the airport she cries all over his shirt.

"Foolish American woman." His eyes glisten. "First I

want to steal Tess away from you crazy American. But now, I give her to you, like my love." But he reluctantly loosens his hold on Tess, who carries his sweaty scent to Donna. Tess refuses to let go of his neck, bringing the three of them close. "I tell you now. Su Lin. I know her. Captain thinks he father. Su Lin not tell him, she's afraid he kill. Tess born with Korean father." He looks at her. "But Su Lin had GI father, yes. Captain right about that." He smiles. "You not forget me. Send pictures from your country."

Flying toward America, Donna feels the shape of Tess fitting into her arm, against her hip, but the weight of the congealed memory begins to disperse into the sun and water spreading behind them. This child she did not want takes up all the chambers of her mind, though she sees that the plane is but an insect over the water.

Pushing herself free of Donna, Tess rummages in the bags of toys and the impressive doll tumbles out onto the empty seat. Donna suspects there are no ashes under its bodice. Tess licks a souvenir stamp, gluing it over the rice dolls' window, and gives Donna a sly glance.

Chalk Line

THE NEIGHBOR HAS RUN AN EIGHT-FOOT board fence down the property line; the wife run a chalk line down the center of the house. Now I'm stuck on the side that looks out on a wall of utility-grade lumber. The wife says he put up the fence to hide the things I scatter around the yard. Though she's happy enough to have me fix everything in the county. She must know I need parts. But from her side she can watch the garden grow. And from one window she can even see the bus stop. I tell you, I'm feeling hemmed in. Natcherly, it's no chalk line clean down the whole house. It's only right there in the doorway into the kitchen. She leaves me standing in the hall to get my dinner shoved out to me like I was at a drive-in restaurant. I got no way to turn. Can't go this way, can't go that. Can't go back because they don't make that time machine yet that lets you into the past. Can't go up, cause God broke out all the rungs to the ladder way back in Bible times. Can't go down, because we do soon enough. Soon enough and she can erase her chalk line, move someone else in here

and start over, sweet as a kitten, then chalk him out and
pen him up too. This house is almost slam up against the
chain-link fence of D. B. Anderson and Sons, Hauling and
Storage. So, I can't really turn out the back of the house
either, not with any elbowroom. I can go in and out the
front door, though. She gives me leave through the center
hall and the old parlor. I could play the piano if I took a
mind. So, I got the back bathroom. Means I get the shower
and she gets her bubble baths. I miss resting in hot bathwater. And she says I don't bathe frequent enough to suit
her. I get the little bedroom plus the spare room filled with
her years of cardboard boxes. I don't have the faintest notion
what she's put in those boxes crowding my tools. I'm not
of a mind to look. Parlor's mine and I guess I could claim
the pantry, too, by this map of hers. But I see her out of
the corner of my eye, running across the hall in and out of
there like the mice she's at war with. I'm not gonna raise
a fuss. She makes my dinners. She's an awful good cook.

"Marvin, you getting ready to go out?"

Yes, she still talks to me, almost like normal. I never
did find out item by item what she was up to, I never
learned the rules. I'm just like one of those rats they put in
mazes; just one day almost ever which way I turned I was
like to get shocked. No reasons. Too bad. I woke up one day
last week and there it was. I would like to have leave to
move my stamp collection to the parlor. I sure do miss it.

"Marvin? You take this letter for me, please?"

See, she still expects me to do things right by her. She
don't expect me to dump her letters in the ditch or pull the
stamps off. Her pastor told me the other day that marriage
is based on trust. I think he suspects something, but I don't
think she told him nothing. It would make her seem
crotchety in his eyes. And she don't want that. She's got
him mixed up with the Lord Good God himself. He's sure
come between us. She gets so high and mighty with religion,

she's not fit company and can't stand her own husband. That's not what the Bible tells women, to my mind.

"Marvin. Yoo hoo. I heard you come downstairs."

And there she is. Good-looking for an old biddy. Her pastor thinks so too. He can have her and send his soul to Hell over a sixty-year-old prune. I bet she stole that chalk right out of the Sunday School room. "Yes, Aggie, you hard old woman, I'm right here." Now that would make the angels sore. To lose one of their own stalwart preachers over some old bag.

"Did I hear you call me an old bag? Do you really think that's any way to earn yourself a reconciliation?"

Hm. She couldn't of heard me; I wasn't talking to her. She's been talking to somebody, though. Reconciliation. More like a lawyer's term than a preacher's, seems to me. She's got the phone in her half. Hard to tell who she yaks to about this. You'd think this line down the middle of our lives would mean she'd leave me be. No sir. I got just as much trouble or more, it seems.

"I wrote to Rose Ellen. I know you'll look anyway to see who it's to."

"Your sister gonna come visit again?"

"She's welcome whenever she wants a place to stay."

Aggie complains I've not been kind to her relations. That's not true. I've always done for them. "If you Frost girls'd ever learned to be nice to a man, you'd all have a place to stay."

"Marvin, that's just all I'm gonna hear out of you about my little sister. And besides, she can stay with Faye all the time she wants. And it's both of them that're coming. They're my sisters and they are always welcome."

"You tell 'em?"

"Tell them what?"

"You know. About your little game here. About your keeping your husband penned up in his own house."

"Don't be silly. You can come and go as you please."

"Well, I think I'll go sit a spell in the kitchen, have me a cup of coffee."

"Don't you start up again. Don't you set foot in that kitchen. You want coffee, I'll bring you some out."

"Give me that letter. I'm goin' now."

And there on the envelope, Aggie's stuck on a Great Smoky Mountains, gray, issued 1934. Beside it a seven-cent Washington Bicentennial. And, there above Rose Ellen's name is the 1926 Ericsson Memorial, the purple beauty. Ericsson, he invented the ship screw propeller my book says, sits on a throne. A naked lady is above him, throwing her cloak up over her head like a cloud. They're looking so calm, so grand, pasted down right by Aggie's hen scratch writing; I think I won't be able to talk. "Aggie, where'd you get these stamps?" She knows my hands are about ready to reach out and pinch her throat shut.

"Well, if you are so selfish you can't spare me twenty-two cents, I guess we know why you've lost your pillow and table privileges," she whispers like butter wouldn't melt.

"You stay out of my stamps. You just..."

"Oh, don't get carried away, Marvin. I know you're collecting them. I just took them off the ones where you had whole sheets full. I didn't take them out of the book or out of those little pockets. Can't really say you couldn't spare them. There's a difference between collecting and hoarding. One of each, I'd say that's collecting. Any more, I'd say it's trying to lay up treasure. Foolishness."

"I don't have to put up with this." That's it perzactly. I don't have to put up with it. She sees I'm thinking about it.

"Marvin, you leave this house and it's abandonment. You'll never see one stick nor one penny out of this place; you lose it all. You lay a hand on me and it's assault. Wife beating. So, big talk, I just don't know what you can do about it."

I see she's sure been getting advice from somewhere.

I look back down to Ericsson. He built that ship, the Monitor. What defense would he make now against Aggie? I see he died in 1889, it's right here on the stamp. He can't help no one now. Then it comes on me. Just as plain as that chalk mark Aggie's refreshed after her vacuuming. That lady, making that pretty cloud over the shipbuilder has got nothing better to do now than to come visiting me. I'm going up to my room to wait for her.

"Where are you going with my sis's letter? You can keep your old stamps if you got a twenty-two center to lick on. But you'd better not read my private correspondence, mister."

I don't answer. I go down the hall and up the stairs. I don't think about Aggie making her noises on her side of the house any more than I think of the mice hightailing inside the walls.

I'm just thinking about that lady. She's naked and dressed all at the same time, in an evening gown and in her nightgown. All at once. She's ready for whatever.

I think I've been dozing 'cause I hear Aggie's voice all of a sudden like a saw blade hit a nail.

"Oh, my Lord. Oh, my gracious. That's my baby sister getting off the bus. Marvin. Marvin. Hurry. Run out and carry Rose Ellen's suitcase. Oh my Lord. I thought she was coming next month." And the screen door bangs.

I think I must have been dreaming about Ericsson's Lady. But I get on down and out on the porch about the time Aggie's helping Rose Ellen with enough baggage to keep a dozen women busy for two years just opening it all up.

"Well, Marvin, you do look wonderful," says Rose Ellen, expecting me to say she does. She knows that when the light's right, anybody'd think she was thirty-five instead of fifty-three. "You are so lionine," she says, dumping her bags and giving me a smooch right out here on the front porch.

Aggie is like a spark plug and Rose Ellen a hot wire touched to her. "Let's not make a spectacle for the neighbors," says the wife. Though the neighbor's not likely to get an eyeful through that fence. I bet he put it up to hide his own goings-on.

"We thought you was coming next month, Rose Ellen." Then, seeing Aggie looking cross at me, I go on, "Not that there's any reason to hold off with a good thing." This causes Rose Ellen to give me another smooch and Aggie to look cross at both of us. If her pastor ever saw that look he'd think she's got a ticket for Hell for sure. And when she tells me to put Rose Ellen's stuff in the little bedroom I musta got a smile on my face, cause Aggie just trots right past me like I was Jack the Ripper.

"I just always wonder," says Rose Ellen, "I was just saying to Faye, 'How is it that Aggie got the one with good looks, you got the one who leaves you with property, and I got two of them—but they were one just a weasel and the other just a louse.'" Rose Ellen's here to heal her love troubles again, no doubt.

I lug the bags up the back steps and into the little bedroom and take note of that letter to Rose Ellen still lying on the dresser. I was supposed to send it off this morning and here she is; I don't know what to do with it. I guess I'll stick it in one of these suitcases so she can read it when she gets home. And I guess I won't begrudge her my stamps. A woman like her might notice how fine they look. I take a look at Ericsson's monument again. Then my dream comes back to me. In my dream that woman was looking to cut my hair. She was in my dream cutting off my hair saying... Well, who can remember what's said in dreams.

I open Rose Ellen's suitcase and right on top is a nightie that wouldn't be fit for nobody but a stone statue to wear. It surprises me so much I hold it up and I can see the bed and the chair right through it. Thinking that Rose Ellen would wear the thing, makes me drop it like it was burning. The nightie sprawls all over, yards of it. Like the woman in the dream. And, whether I like it or not, I hear what the lady told me in the dream, with those scissors in her hand,

"Marvin, we're gonna cut your hair so you'll fit. Your hair's too tall." Silly. And she was standing barefoot on a coffin. I don't think it's meant for people to remember their dreams. I think I better take another nap and wake up luckier next round.

"Marvin," Aggie calls. "We're waiting dinner on you, honey." Honey. I must of dreamed that too. But I get myself up and get down the stairs and she's pointing the way to the dining room like I'm the Prince of Egypt. I look around, just to make sure it's as I remembered it a week ago. "Sit down, Marvin, and lead us in grace."

I don't feel much of a grace coming on, but I do my imitation of her pastor. It gives me fun, and she's not sure whether or not I'm playing her straight.

Come to think on it, I may have some notion now why she's seen fit to corral me in my own house. I look up at Rose Ellen. She's puzzled; she thinks I sound like I got religion. I give her knee a little squeeze just to keep her more mixed up. Then I squeeze Aggie's knee just to see what she's gonna tolerate with Sis here. Lord, I think they both like it. My grace must have been a powerful one.

Too bad I only got two hands and a plate full of chicken besides. "My dad used to say," I offer, since these hens are quiet and looking at me, "he used to say, boy, you better watch out what you pray for. 'Cause you might get it." Don't know how I come to think of that now. They look at me like I'm crazy. I've never seen them so quiet. But I don't let on, and pretty soon they're in a gossip so thick I make a little chair out of my paper napkin, put toothpicks in a stuffed olive and set it there like a mouse. They don't miss me getting up from the table.

While I got the chance, I make three trips from the living room to the parlor, depositing my stamps and paraphernalia where I can get at them.

Then behind me Rose Ellen says, "Let's take tea in here, Aggie, so we can sit with Marvin while he does his stamps.

Oh, Marvin," she squeals like a girl, "how could you make that cute little chair and kitty cat right under our noses?"

"Marvin's real good making things," Aggie admits. She grudges it too.

I don't tell Rose Ellen it was a mouse. No sense pushing my luck with trifles.

"Joanie says Lisa Rose is just dying for a dollhouse," Rose Ellen says. I try to remember whether she had Joanie with the weasel or the louse. Funny how things goes out of your head. "Oh, Marvin, why don't you make her one? You're so clever with your hands."

And, well. It just seems like the thing to do. I start scratching out plans and doodling. Lisa Rose is the only little girl in the family. So I'll only have to make one. I can see it. I'll make little picture frames, and put in some stamps. That'll look pretty. Not common ones. Some handsome ones. Maybe I'll put that Ericsson over the mantel. I'll make the fireplace of little stones. I'll make two staircases cut through the upper floor. I want these rooms to be like a real house. No painted stairsteps and doors. The little dolls will be able to go all over. Tiny hinges. I might have to send off for them. Everything's going to open and close for real.

I'm busy drawing up plans on butcher paper till Aggie calls me for bed. Now this, I think, will be interesting. But things just go along like we're putting on a show for Rose Ellen. Aggie's already hauled my clothes back to the big bedroom and doesn't say a word. And she's reasonable as any man expects of a wife once the lights is out. I think, well, wait'll sister Faye arrives here on the fourteenth and Aggie'll turn sweet as Samson's honey.

But things is never as simple as you'd want. We wake up to another maze. I hear they do this to the rats, too. Soon's they learn a maze, they switch the walls around. By the time I get breakfast, peaceful, at the kitchen table where it belongs, and then set up my dollhouse manufacture in the spare room, it's all changed again.

Aggie comes traipsing up to me and says, "Rose Ellen's so upset. She's cried her eyes out all night. She needs some peace and quiet. I told her you won't step foot on her side of the house."

"Which side of the house is that?"

"Now don't wear my patience, Marvin. You know very well what side. The side you just come from."

First I was locked out from Aggie, now I'm locked in with her so as not to disturb baby sister. I go to get my stamps from the old parlor, to pack them back to the living room, and you never heard the likes of screeching females from both sides. Aggie and Rose Ellen tell me to stay where I belong. Here I am again, me on one side and my stamps on the other. I don't go on about it, as it does appear to me Rose Ellen is a little under the weather. She comes home to Aggie after ever tumble. I spect that retired Marine wasn't all she bargained for. At least we don't have to add him to the list with the other two. And, I'm just as happy to oblige Aggie by keeping distance from Rose Ellen. I guess that means Aggie does see something in me she wants to keep for herself.

Course, from this side of the house I can see the bus stop. And I know they'll let me in the spare room cause they want that dollhouse for little Lisa. Or for themselves. I heard them like they was shopping for curtains, digging through Aggie's material scraps. Well, I won't give that house up as easy as this one.

But I did think yesterday when Rose Ellen come that she was going to make for something different. But two women is just two of the same. Come the fourteenth I'm getting on the bus when Faye gets off it. Feel sorry for that shipbuilder, with that stone woman standing over his head for all the rest of time.

"Marvin."

Now what could she want?

"Marvin?" she runs in whispering. "Pastor's coming

over at two. I want you to take Rose Ellen downtown, get her out of here. I just can't have her butting in while I got my visit with Pastor."

Nope. Whenever I got it figured she changes the lines. "That'll be fine," I say. "I got to pick up some finish nails and a glass cutter for little Lisa's house."

"Well, good. Remember her birthday is in September. I bet you don't even remember. So that gives you plenty of time to get it all painted and prettied."

That little niece might be all grown up before I get the dollhouse done. I'm taking my time. And these old gals won't get their hands on it 'til I'm good and ready. They can turn me any which way, block me any which way, but the little house, oh Lord, the house is going to have a polished banister, and wallpaper colored by patterns carved on the eraser ends of pencils, and, yeah, and a pantry fitted up with little preserves and a family of mice, I see it now. I believe I'll make a four-poster bed. Maybe a canopy. That dollhouse, the one they'll really want the run of, they won't be able to get hold of it. Yeah, a canopy. Then Ericsson, that poor devil, he'll just have to keep that woman of his spreading her coat over his head forever. I'll have my own overhang with the canopy of my own making.

"Marvin," Aggie shakes my sleeve, "are you listening? Marvin, don't you see, when you ignore me it just keeps us alienated? It just keeps an invisible wall between us."

Who's filling her up with this stuff? The roof. Now that's to be considered. Dollhouses I seen at the County Fair don't trouble enough to make good-looking little shingles. With every part, you gotta keep scale in mind.

When the Pie
Was Opened

GRANDPA IS RAKING THE YARD AND RAV-
ing at the cedars. One because Grandma told him to, the
other because the Lord is telling him to. *"Like a basket full
of birds, their houses are full of treachery,"* we can hear him
through the open window. *"Why did I come forth from this
womb to see toil and sorrow, and spend my days in shame?"*
It's not that he hates raking that much, it's just that whatever
he does, God is always interrupting him and getting him
into conversation. I don't believe any of that stuff.

"Well, she was a nice woman," my grandmother says,
ignoring Grandpa's voice. "She measured the sunflowers
every season, kept a record how high each year got, and
saved the seeds of the tallest. She had this house," she said,
flinging her arm toward Purla's little homemade house out
back, her apron flying up like a wing. Then lowering her
voice, my grandma says, "Three breasts, and not one good
man in the whole lot of them."

I figure she's just trying to tickle my interest in something silly so I won't dwell on the fact my grandpa has really

gone crazy from talking too much to the Lord all the time, or to the predicament she finds herself in with the jewel box.

"Not one of them a man worth shooting," she says. I don't know which she wants to distract me from, but whichever it is, she's trying to make chatter out of this neighbor of hers who just died off, leaving Grandma sitting here talking to herself.

So I say, "What do you mean, three breasts?"

She smiles and moves a lump of cheese in her mouth in one easy motion. She's an efficiency expert. She thinks she's grabbed my interest this time. I don't think anybody was even allowed to say the word breast when she was a girl. I can't stand listening to her long, though. Dumped here by my mom while she goes off chasing that guy who calls her Babe and is too fat for his motorcycle, I don't listen too much. I've been here thirty-two days; I'm keeping track. I've only been able to see Gary twice in all this time because they won't let him visit me. It was so cold in the woods the last night he came, neither of us had any fun. Tonight, when he sneaks down here, I've decided we'll use Purla's house. No one will know.

What's Grandma saying now? I can never pay attention to her all the way through her stories. Except for twice. Once when she told about my mother being on the radio, and once when she herself was thrown out a second-story window. Here I am, sixteen years old and having to waste my whole summer this way, because I had the luck to get pregnant and they think they have to hide me away until we get this baby born.

"She had three," she says, taking a big bite off a dill pickle.

"I thought you got those pickles for me," I say.

"I did. But you already eat your ice cream; you don't have no use for the pickles." She thinks she's pretty funny.

"How do you know?" Lying on my back on the floor, I

keep checking to see how big this mountain in the middle of me is getting. I've passed up the cabbages in my grandmother's garden, that's for sure.

"Lord, I grew up with her. She died before her time, I guess; though I'm surprised she lived this long. I saw her when I was a child, seven years old. They laid her, naked and new born, on the bed and showed all the women. Three little buttons. Not exactly even. I never forgot because Mae decided the baby was a devil. All the women were pulling on Mae and they say if I hadn't of bit her leg, she woulda killed Purla."

"You saved her life?"

"Guess so." She does think so, too, because she looks satisfied with herself.

"Then how come you couldn't save her this time?"

"What do you mean?"

"She died, didn't she?"

"Supposed to die. Everyone's *supposed* to die."

"Now you sound like Grandpa."

"I don't mean it the way that fool says it."

"Do you believe him at all?"

She pushes those caterpillar eyebrows together until they kiss on her face and then she separates them again before she says, "I think my life has meant more to me because I always knew I had saved another one before I could hardly even read."

"Yeah, but do you believe any of that stuff God tells Grandpa?"

"Don't tell him too much that's not in the Bible," she says, but I still don't believe it. "People. You'll find out. People always takes things for signs. They never see nothing straight, it's always a sign of something that's got nothing to do with it. Now, take Purla for example." See, Grandma won't talk about anything upsetting us. Only about the parts that don't matter anymore. "She looked like a sign to lots of folks. After Mae calmed down, old Peter Wilson asks to be let in, and he tells everybody that child Purla is an Emblem of God. Peter had teeth that looked like he'd been chewing bark and bushes all his life, stringy blond hair, but I can tell you, there was something handsome about that man. Something you were just glad he walked in the room. I'd always run and sit on his lap. He'd comb tangles outa my hair with a little bitty comb he had in his pocket. Never hurt me. He was not like most men, but he sure was one they all listened to. And he said, 'That child's an emblem.' That settled it."

"What's an emblem?" I think I know, but sometimes I just ask questions because it's expected. I am measuring my belly with my fingers like spider-walks. Almost six spider-walks over this mountain from one side of the floor to the other. I wish I had looked closer at Purla, but Mom and I hardly ever came here.

"Pull your shirt down. An emblem's a sign. Of course, I never thought she was much of one myself. Well, it's a sign that's not just giving you a way to figure something out, but like a special writing direct sent from Heaven."

See, why do I ask her anything? She's no good at explaining anything. She just starts drawing in the air. And Mom packed me up so fast, I don't even have any books with me. Of course, I bet they think I got pregnant from reading. You keep to yourself too much, they like to say. You read too much; you'll spoil your eyesight. Even so, they won't let me see Gary. What a laugh. "Why didn't you believe Peter Wilson?" I ask. Actually, I haven't read a new book in a long time; I haven't felt like it. I just keep reading my old ones over again.

"Cause I saved that baby's life. If there was a sign, I guess I wanted it to be my teethmarks in the back of Mae's leg."

"Why didn't Peter think so?"

"Oh, I don't know that he didn't. When I was fifteen, he asked me to marry him."

"How old was he?"

"Sixty, I guess."

"Dumb."

"It was just foolishness. I was already courting your grandpa. Soon after that Peter Wilson was found with a six-inch blade sticking in his throat."

"Is he the one that taught Grandpa to listen to the Lord?"

"No!" she closes her mouth over a cold biscuit oozing her apple butter. She looks mad, like she's finally realizing that whatever she talks about really just reminds us of the stuff she thinks we can't talk about. Or else, she's suddenly forgotten it all, and is just thinking with her tongue, her mouth all crammed with apple butter.

She looks at me and thinks she'd better keep talking so I don't have time to think.

"When I was your age," she says, glaring at me, "I remember people had pretty much forgotten that Purla was an Emblem. She was more like a child that sprung up from the garden, just something budding. Folks didn't think nothing of stroking the front of her dress when they caught her in the field. No one ever harmed her. Then when I was married and Purla was becoming a woman, all of a sudden no one recalled anything about those breasts. Everyone forgot."

"I bet."

"Forgetting is better than you think. And happens more than you think. It was like a shame all of a sudden clouding her. And she was a sweet thing, no one wanted her to be burdened. What was one thing in a child was another in a young girl, a woman."

"You never forgot."

"Of course I never forgot. I tell you, ever since I saved Purla's life it was like I was carrying her little heart in my hands and could never put it down. Lord, I'm tired, and I guess it was time to put it down. I will have some rest, some hours to tend my own."

"What?"

"What's what? That's the sound Tom Fool makes rapping on the door." She always thinks she's so superior to me because she says all those dumb things from when she was a kid. She wakes up her caterpillars on her face again. I shut my eyes so she won't have anyone to watch her.

"Lord, how things changed for her," she starts saying in a louder voice. "She told me all her secrets," she says, smug as that tattle-tale Reverend Connors that comes around here to fight with Grandpa and gossip with Grandma and look at me. "Once when she was about your age, and she was a good girl," I know what she's implying, "a boy says 'Here's two bits if you let me see them.' She didn't pay no attention. Then he says, 'Two bits and show you mine.' He hands her the quarter, shows her what he's got. It's nothing unusual, and Purla gives him back the quarter and walks away." My grandmother's joke. Ha ha. "But those kind pestered her all the time."

"I need a new bra," I say, mine's pinching me. I think it's a good thing I don't have three.

"You know what? That was only a nickel he handed her in the first place." Ha ha.

"Christina Rose, sit in a chair"—my grandpa scares both of us—"*And I saw the woman, drunk with the blood of saints and the blood of the martyrs of Jesus.*" He tricks us by coming in the front door instead of the back, as he usually does. I get up and move to a chair. I really didn't look drunk. Grandma moves to sweep her crumbs from the table and set a clean place for Grandpa's lunch.

"Your dinner is ready, John," my grandmother says. "Did I ever tell you, Tina, about the time your mommy was on the radio?"

"No," I say. I've got sense enough to know that she doesn't want to talk about Purla in front of Grandpa. I don't think it's just because it's breast talk, either. I think there's no safe conversation possible in this house anymore. So I pretend I haven't heard about the radio. I don't mind.

"Well, your mom. . ."

"Where's my coffee?" says Grandpa.

"Right here. Your mom was just ten years old when the radio people visited her school to find the smartest child. They were talent scouting." Grandma just keeps talking while Grandpa mumbles his grace. "And you know Darlene was always the one who could talk her way out of Hell itself."

Grandpa opens his eyes, raises an eyebrow at Grandma and stabs the tines of his fork into the leftover pot roast. She runs and gets him the last of those seven jars of strawberry jam we made the first sickening day I got here. That'll keep him from starting in. He punches in the paraffin seal, pulls it out and licks it.

"For a spirit of harlotry has led them astray," he says then, *"and they have left their God to play the harlot. They sacrifice on the tops of the mountains, and make offerings upon the hills, under oak, poplar, and terebinth, because their shade is good. Therefore your daughters play the harlot."* He's getting going, looking at the ceiling, but Grandma tries to cut him off, getting as loud as he is.

"That girl," says Grandma, "she was picked from all eight grades and three different schools in the county."

Grandpa stops for a minute, looks over at her and says, *"...and your brides commit adultery,"* and he shuts up and starts eating.

"They wanted someone for 'Grady Grimes and Father Time's Saturday Hour Sublime.'" I can tell she's trying to sound like the radio.

"I never heard of it," I say.

"It was the most popular show on the radio then. Everybody listened." Grandpa's listening, too, like he's going to stick her with his fork if she says something wrong.

"She was so good, they had her on again and again. She could just talk about everything. People started writing letters and penny postcards saying, 'Ask the little girl what does she think about this?' and 'Can I have a picture of Little Darlene?' and someone even offered to pay her five dollars a week just to come and visit them on Sundays. It got to be any problem nobody knew what to do, they'd write in and ask Darlene. One day, Purla says to John, 'How come if the Lord speaks to you, John, Darlene's the one on the radio with the answers?' " I can see she's decided to start in on him, since he wasn't going to bother us. I don't know why.

"She did not," says my grandfather, trying to quote Purla instead of God. "She said, 'How come with the Lord speaking direct to you, those fools just want to hear something a little child makes up?' "

He doesn't look too much like the old prophets that God used to talk to. He's big, but sort of skinny, with a puffy face, like he has no bones in his head and no hair on it. I bet if he looked more like the hairy, bony guys in the Bible, people'd listen to him. Maybe. Grandma suddenly looks like she made a mistake; she didn't mean to get into it about Purla with Grandpa. Her eyes are as shiny as the beetles in her garden trying to get away from the sun when you pull the rock back. She just pulled back some rock on her thoughts and her whole face is bugs. Grandpa's whole mind is bugs. I've got to get out of here.

Grandma keeps on talking; that's always her cure for everything, just look for the stupidest things that don't matter and talk them to death. Obviously, Purla matters a whole lot to both of them. Maybe I'll name my baby Purla and it will have three breasts. Only joking down there. Don't come out a freak, Baby. I think I've decided to keep you for sure. If I can figure out how to keep you without Grandpa and Grandma keeping me. "Darlene," says Grandma, "could have been richer and more famous than Shirley Temple."

"Why wasn't she?"

"*Because God will not permit his daughters to become Folly,*" says Grandpa, "*Folly is noisy, she is wanton and knows no shame. She sits at the door of her house, she takes a seat on the high places of the town,*" Grandpa stands up, "*calling to those who pass by, who are going straight on their way, 'Whoever is simple, let him turn in here!' And to him who is without sense she says, 'Stolen water is sweet and bread eaten in secret is pleasant.' But he does not know that the dead are there, that her guests are in the depths of Sheol."* Have to hand it to Grandpa, for knowing a lot of Bible. I wonder how he can keep it all memorized. I hate to memorize anything. ROY G BIV. Every Good Boy Does Fine. The circumference of a circle is $2\pi r$. That must be me. I'm a circle. I'm a pie. Four and twenty blackbirds baking in me. Shall I call you Blackbird, Baby? Don't worry.

Grandpa storms out the back door and Grandma hollers after him, "Would you trim that hedge now, John; I can't see nothing to the east."

He kicks over the can of scraps for the chickens and it rolls down the steps. He leaves the mess to Grandma. And she'll give it to me.

"I'm going to throw up," I say.

"You're past the throwing-up stage, girl. Use the dust-pan to clean up those scraps with. Then rinse it off."

"Why didn't Mom get to be rich and famous?" Then I'd be rich and famous. Not stuck here. Not pregnant. No offense, Baby.

"Because just when things was getting going, there was a terrible tragedy. That whole radio station burned up and Grady Grimes just couldn't get it started again. Grady was there when it happened and got terrible burned. It disfigured him," she says like she's reading a letter. It's amazing she could have left out that part of the story the first time she told me. She really has no brains.

Then those beetle eyes see I'm lying on the floor again. "After you get done, throw it all to the chickens. Then pick some beans. Why haven't you picked any beans yet today? You getting lazy?" Grandma's idea of lazy is if you are not picking, chopping, or scrubbing at something. I get up and go out the back door. "Don't slam," she says. I'm not going to say any of that stuff to my baby.

Grandpa nailed up chicken wire to the porch and sweet

peas are all over it. I pick sweet peas before I think about that garbage or those beans. I pick all the pink ones, then all the purples. There's one I can't decide if it's a pink or purple. I put it in my mouth. Then I realize what I've done and I'm glad no one can see me. Maybe Baby likes sweet peas. I eat another purple, just in case. Eating for two. Then I pick the orange ones, then red-scarlet, then the dark red-magenta-maroon. There's only two of them. Even seeds will give you least of what's nicest. I leave the white ones on the vines and bring the bouquet in the house.

"I thought you was picking beans."

"I got these first."

"You're supposed to mix them up. Did you get those scraps to the chickens yet? Never mind, I'll do it myself."

I follow her out of the house and watch her kneel down before the peelings.

She goes down to offer them to the chickens, but I hang around in the yard. I've got work to do before Gary shows up tonight. I've got to see how hard it is to get in Purla's house so we can figure it out in the dark. Grandma says no one can go in that house while "the estate's tied up." Estate. What a joke. Grandpa owns the land. No one's going to cart off Purla's cardboard house or old dresses. Maybe her bras.

She can't see me now; Grandpa's in the garage. Going back in here, where the vines are higher than her house and behind those nothing but woods, no one can see. I'm scared they'll catch me. And scared—even though I don't believe in those things—of seeing Purla's ghost.

It's nothing to get in; I just swing my fat self in through the little kitchen window. It's the size of a back porch, but the sink is really too big, like a laundry room. The stove is on legs. There are hardly any dishes; most of them have little faded roses. They're cute. Gary and I could use those, but I'll leave them alone. It's probably bad luck to eat on a dead person's dish. No, probably not. They'd have to break too many dishes if that were true. But it might not be too good for babies not yet born.

There's only one other room, not counting the bathroom, which I'll skip. She slept in her living room. The bed has a rose satin cover; boy, what a surprise. The closet just has her old dresses and shoes. Wow. Buttons. Thousands. Jars full of them.

The drawers are great, stuffed with interesting junk. I wish I could look at every single thing, but I'd better get back. Look at this book; must have belonged to one of her babies "that died awful deaths, poor little things." They scribbled all over their "When the pie was opened, The birds began to sing, Wasn't that a dainty dish to set before the king." How do they expect kids to like stories where the birds sing about themselves getting eaten up? I wonder if the kid knew it was going to die when it scribbled on this. Look at this. Great. A little bag of money. Funny old coins. Nickels with V's on them; Indian-head pennies. I'd better leave them here. You try to spend these and the cops'll be right down on you, I bet. I'll just take a few for kicks to give to Gary. If Grandma doesn't check my pockets when I go back. I'm feeling strange. I'd better go. I'll be missed.

I can still jump Purla's little fence with my big tummy. She hardly had any more space—yard or house—than the chickens have.

"Where you been?"

"Didn't you tell me I've got to get air?"

"Just step aside here. While I chop this slug in two." She slices up a slug with the point of her shovel. "Blame things eat my garden."

"Ick."

"Get in the house. If you don't get some lunch pretty soon you'll run right up against supper."

"How did Purla die?"

"In her bed."

"I mean what from?"

"Natural causes," she says, like someone who doubts it. I really wonder if Grandpa isn't crazier right now because he thinks Grandma smothered Purla. Or poisoned her.

"Did they do an autopsy? Have an inquest?" I ask seriously.

"Now what have you been reading? Course not. Just an old woman, sweet old thing, dies in her bed. No one bothers with that."

"Lucky."

"Lucky she lived as long as she did and had good people to take care of her."

"Why'd she move way up here, live in the same place you do? Isn't that pretty strange? How'd she get her money?"

"Only way she could. Course it's not strange. She was so grateful, she saved up all her money and bought a grave plot. Said she didn't want nobody have to give her land for her bones."

"Do you think she's glad to be a skeleton? Do you think she's a skeleton yet? No, she wouldn't be a skeleton yet, would she? I mean when all her skin and insides rot off, she'll be a regular, normal skeleton."

"Tina, don't talk that way. You put me in mind of a crazy person. You got to think good thoughts for that child."

"I just mean," I'm shouting at her, "when she's a skeleton she won't have three breasts anymore."

"God Almighty. You want a sandwich? You want me to heat up that soup? You want me to fix you some eggs?"

"Maybe she didn't have three anymore, by the time she died."

"Yes, she did."

"How do you know?" I know I got to her this time. Those beetle eyes are looking for a rock to hide under.

"I know. I prepared the body before the undertaker come and got her." And, like she's been aching to tell somebody, "Some old women," she says as though she's not included, "their bosoms fall like they's half-empty sacks. Two of hers did that. But the one that was more toward the middle, it was more wrinkled up, like it was rotten." And she thinks I'm gross. I lay back down on the floor.

"Get up. Before your grandpa comes back in here. You

want tuna fish? You want roast? Want me to cut you up some of that pot roast and make you a sandwich? You gotta eat something."

"I might throw up."

"Don't expect me to believe that. That goes away after the first few weeks."

"Who found her?"

"I did. No, I guess it was your grandpa. Well, I really don't recall. Don't matter none anyhow."

I think she killed Purla. I'm going to find out. "How'd you find her? Day or night?" I could probably be a good detective.

"Day, naturally. I was bringing her some warm cornbread. She'd been feeling poorly. I knew she wasn't much for cooking anyway."

"I thought Grandpa found her first."

"Yes, that's right. He went over to see if she needed something from up town."

"Both of you couldn't have found her." I feel like what's his name with the pipe, catching her in her contradiction. Sherlock Holmes. Don't worry, Baby, I won't name you Sherlock.

"Pay attention to what I say." She sounds exasperated. "I was on my way over with the cornbread. Your grandpa had already gone over to see what she wanted from town. He come out of the house before I could get across the yard." This is good. It's like reading a book. She wants me to think Grandpa was in that house first so I won't suspect her of killing Purla, not just finding her. "What you going to eat?" she says.

"Ice cream."

"You already ate it all."

"Tuna fish. No. Roast beef and cheese." It makes her so happy; I should probably ask for tuna fish on top.

"I ever tell you about the time I fell out the second-story window?"

"No," I say. I have to soften her up, get her talking,

then spring a question on her and see if she admits she killed Purla. Psychology. If I can get her to confess, she'll stop bugging me about getting pregnant.

"Well, I was just a young thing. A man comes into the cafe where I work and every day orders steak and eggs. Every time he leaves me twenty-five cents. Name of Ethan."

"Where's Grandpa?"

"Hm? Oh, he was laid up and couldn't work. Anyway, one day Ethan says to me he'd done Sunday Sections from here to Cincinnati. You should have heard him talk. He had a real nasal voice, but everything he said sounded like it was a song. He said his work was always showing up in the ro-to-gravure."

"What's that?"

"Sunday pictures."

"Funnies."

"No. Special things." She never gets a joke. "Pretty things," she says because of what's coming next. I know. I'm never going to tell my baby the same story twice. I'll just take it to movies. "Ethan says he can use me to show off some real jewels he's got to photograph; and he wants to do a serious, heart-touching series on the working girl; and, he says, if I'm as good in front of the camera as he thinks, he needs me to help him do a story at a snitzy resort."

"How come you didn't know what he was up to?"

"I'd seen plenty of newspapers. I knew the magazine sections was filled with girls and I was as good-looking as any of them I ever saw. I knew that they had to get girls somewhere. And I knew all those quarters meant he was making money. Sometimes he left me thirty-five cents."

"You were smart."

"I was trying. I was just trying to better myself." She means I'm not. "Anyway, Ethan comes to meet me at the back of the kitchen after my shift; I'd changed into my green print rayon dress out of my uniform."

"How do you remember your dress?" I doubt if she really was that pretty.

"I had to wear that thing five years. I sewed it up so many times under the arms I just thought I knew every thread by its first name."

"How'd he get you to go to his house?"

"It wasn't his house; it was his artist's studio."

Grandpa goes banging into the garage, *"I will remove its hedge!"* he yells, coming out with the clippers. Who's he think he's kidding? Does he think everything is in the Bible?

"Same difference," I say, forgetting for a minute I'm trying to soften her up to get her to confess.

"Not at all. He takes me up this narrow flight of steps, wiring dangling down, looking like it's gonna catch fire any minute. It don't look too prosperous. He gets a little fresh going up the steps; they'll do it every chance they get climbing stairs. I'm getting sorry I come. I think I might have misjudged. But then he takes the padlock off this old scarred-up door and inside it's white and light and real nice. Lots of equipment around. He unlocks a drawer and takes out a tray of jewels. So I know I done the right thing."

I think I just felt the baby move. Did you move, Baby?

"He was an artist. He says he's gotta do this special booklet on these jewels and he wants me to put these big gaudy bracelets on my ankles. Wear them on my legs instead of my arms. I swear. You know people get paid for acting a fool. He gets to work, propping, arranging. It weren't no time for modesty. He wasn't even putting my face in the picture, just my legs. It was going to be a special book put out just for certain rich customers. My face is in the dark and my legs is bright as candles."

"This is disgusting. What a pervert."

"No, it wasn't like that. He wasn't even thinking about me. He started powdering here, streaking a little vaseline on there—you know, so in the picture some parts would show up more than others. It tickled and I was trying so hard not to giggle. Then someone bangs on the door, but the photographer says, 'You hold still. Don't ruin my work now.' I did what he says. I've always been a good worker.

Someone's standing behind Ethan, over in the dark, all quiet. All the lights in the whole place is aimed at my anklebone. And those big emerald bracelets on my calf. I hear Ethan talk to the one who's just come in, but I don't hear him get no answers. I shut my eyes against the glare and pretty soon I say, 'Won't you hurry up, this is killing me.' And whoever it was had come in, throws Ethan by the hair into the sink (that's what he told me later, I couldn't see nothing), knocks over the lights and camera. Now no one can see nothing, but I hear crashing and this cutthroat grabs for my leg or for the bracelet. He pulls one of them off me; I know my leg is cut up. I run toward the only sliver of light in the room. I trip—I'm barefooted—and cut my foot, and fly headfirst out that window. Wonder I wasn't killed. Scared the lights outa me. I remember some shouting over my head, then nothing 'til I come to in the hospital."

"Who had done it?"

"No one ever knew."

"What'd the cops do?"

"Police don't care nothing about us. They just make the report."

"Didn't you see the guy that did it?"

"Nope. Ethan neither. He come and see me at the hospital. He gave me flowers, and a Whitman's Sampler, and ten dollars just for that one time. Too bad I was so skinned up and in a cast. They had to shave off most of my hair. I could have made a lot of money working for Ethan."

"He didn't have any idea who came in and hit him?"

"No, he said it was a crazy man. He was hollering so much, Ethan says, and his head bashed against the sink, he couldn't make no sense of it."

"Didn't you know what was going on?"

"I'd like to see a maniac come barging into a dark room at you, you go head first out a window, and see if you keep notes. And that's just what I told the police, too."

"No wonder they couldn't do anything."

"They didn't care. That's one of the reasons Ethan had in mind doing a piece on the working girl. He left town soon after; he must have got another girl in another town. I watched for a story about girls like me, but I never saw one."

"You should have grabbed a handful of the maniac's hair or clothes, then they could have traced him."

"When you think you're going to your end, you're not gathering evidence."

"I am."

She can't just let it go at a sandwich. She's got to give me milk, a dish of canned peaches, and some old green beans. They never eat anything straight from the trees, they turn it into something sticky first. "Thanks," I say, "I don't want these peaches or these beans."

"Maybe you will."

"Maybe it was a friend of Ethan's and they set it up as a robbery or just to be weird and kinky," I suggest.

"Ethan had a big slice up side of his head. Wouldn't of been no friend. I'm sure he was left with a scar all his life. I've kept that in mind; and whenever I get about, I look for men with scars near their eyes. Always thought I'd like to meet up with him again."

"After all that. I'd stay away from him."

"Well. We'd been through something together."

"Something. What'd it feel like, going through a window? How'd you do that?"

"I guess it was a long, narrow window, real low to the floor. There was a dark shade pulled over it; that's probably what saved me from dying. All I could think of was the tower of Babel, like in Sunday School, because I kept hearing a voice above me saying, 'Babylon.' Something about Babylon."

The baby is moving. I'm keeping you, Baby. I've got a whole list of names started. Girls and boys.

"One of the bracelets was lost. I coulda been in trouble from that jewelry store, but the owner told Ethan, 'I want to buy some fancy advertising, not get stuck with bad publicity.' And the jeweler sent me over a pair of beads with his secretary. And another bouquet of flowers. I knew I'd never see so many flowers again until I was dead."

"Let me see the beads."

"Oh, I give them to Purla about fifteen years ago. They're in that thing in the next room."

Uh oh. Now she's admitted something about Purla's jewel box. Three days after I got here, a fat man in suspenders knocked on the door, saying no personal effects were to be removed from that house, and it looked like to him, from his initial investigation, from dust patterns, that a box had been taken from the deceased's dresser. I couldn't figure out who he was or why he'd care, but he sure made Grandma nervous.

Then Grandma said to me, after he left, "Lord, I just brought that thing over here for safekeeping. Now I don't know what to do. I can't put it back. I can't tell him I got it. And I'm sure not letting him get his hands on it."

"Keep it. That's what I'd do," I had said.

But the box has made her so nervous, I think I should just run over there and put it back in its dustprint.

"When did she die exactly?" I ask.

"Two days before you come. The day your mom called and told us you were coming. And told us about the fix you're in. Your grandpa got so agitated, I thought he'd have heart failure. Then this come right on top of it. I told him what the phone call was and he walked right outa the house and found Purla dead. We buried her right away. There wasn't nobody to come from any distance to wait for. We put her in the ground in the morning, got you off the bus that evening."

Thanks a lot. I'm not in any fix. I haven't stolen a jewel box. I'm not a suspect in a big murder. "Who was that man who came to the door that time, trying to get the jewel box?"

"Oh, Purla took him in when he was down. So he thinks

he's got the claim on her goods. Claims he was married to her. Tim Beasley."

"I thought he was from the government or something."

"He acts like it. Ever since he's had a steady job with that warehouse."

"What was he doing in her house anyway?"

"That's a good question, isn't it? I guess he wanted that box. But you know, there's nothing in the world in that box but dime-story play-pretties. Some of that stuff I give her myself."

"Can I look at it?"

"Just leave it be now."

"Why did Purla come here?"

"Because she needed to. She was expecting and had no one to look after her."

All the freaks, I know. Hope it's dark soon. Gary'll be here and I'll have someone to talk to. "What'd Grandpa think?"

"He sent her the ticket." Her beetles glance toward the living room where the box is behind the couch. "Here it is almost your Grandpa's supper time and I'm just a sitting. You go pick those beans and make yourself useful."

I pick beans. I stone a tomato until it's all completely squashed. Out of the corner of my eye, through the plum trees, I think I see someone go in Purla's little house. I run up and put the beans on the porch, "Hey, Grandma, here's the beans. I'm going for a walk."

She runs to the screen door. "Don't be long. Supper pretty soon. There must have been more beans ready than that."

"Nope. I felt their fingers. They need another day or two." I'm learning how to deal with her. I go up the road, then turn in through the cedars. Over the fence again, Baby. I step like a detective. Purla's flowers have gone nuts since she's been dead.

It's pretty hard to see through the screen, the dirt, the

lace. I can see well enough to know it's Grandpa sitting in the rocker and his face is wet with crying. I wonder if he's crying for Purla or if the Lord is complaining to him again. I wonder if he's crying because Purla's dead or because Grandma killed her. Can just barely hear him: "...*drench my couch with weeping.*" Sick. I better get out of here, back by the woods.

Grandma's in the front yard, she starts talking before I get past the mailbox. "Look at this. Diddly squat on this hedge. Left the clippers to rust. Where'd that man go?"

"I think I saw him talking to old Mr. Gerber. I'm not sure." Even Grandpa can't use both Grandma and God down on him. I wonder if I should spring it on her right now. Where he really is, if you really want to know, is he's sitting over in the other woman's house crying. That would break her down.

"Well, supper'll be ready soon's the chicken comes out of the oven and the pie goes in. We're eating high on the hog since you come. But you got to eat for two, don't you?" She's teasing me.

She's going to try to touch my belly; I grab the clippers. "I'll just put these back in the garage."

"Be sure you put them where your grandpa can find them again." She goes back in the house, wiping her hands on her apron, then fanning her face with it, her favorite thing to do, showing how busy she is.

The garage is the only normal place around here. Even though it's dark. The light comes through the cracks in the boards. Everything is stained with years of drops of oil. Regular tools. Regular oil. Regular cardboard boxes. Regular axes and hammers and saws. Regular murder weapons. I've got to get out of here. This place is getting to me; and maybe I should be thinking good thoughts for my baby. I'll hum to you, Baby. I never remember the words. Not like Grandpa. I'll hum and you move once more, please.

You did it. You are a really good baby. Don't worry, I'll

never leave you with the agency. And when you get older, I'll never dump you with your grandma. That would be Mom, of course. She's not so weird. I wish she would have stayed with me this summer. Well, pretty soon Gary will be here. You will call him Dad. That seems funny. He may not stick it out with us anyway. But don't worry about me.

"Supper!" She makes it sound like "Fire!"

Grandpa's already sitting at the table, looking as calm as he can. Maybe he's just thinking about Purla. I bet that's it—I've heard old people do more than you think. I bet Purla was his girlfriend and after all these years Grandma found out. Since she only has two breasts she decided to kill Purla to get her out of the way and to get back at Grandpa. I bet that's it. Couldn't compete with three. Joke.

No, he's just thinking about God. His grace is never going to stop. I keep opening my eyes a slit to see the chicken. She makes really nice potatoes with some stuff in them and a brown crust; I'll give her that. It never sounds like grace, either. He's doing his cartoon animals with heads and horns. Emblems of God for sure.

They make a lot of noise and eat fast. They should eat at the school cafeteria. Except they always make dinner last so long.

"You want some more potatoes?"

"No."

"You want some more. . ."

"No."

"Chicken? You got to be sure you get enough to eat."

"Where's my coffee?" says Grandpa. They're always so much fun I could scream.

"You sit still now, Tina. We got pie."

I have to admit her pies are really good.

"Berries Beth Ann Gerber brought me." She makes berry rhyme with putting a corpse in the ground. "Did Sam Gerber mention to you that Beth Ann brought me some pie berries?"

"Yes. I believe so," says Grandpa. "Said he might have

some more right along." He's slick. But I didn't think the Lord would like this lying. I guess God even likes to avoid trouble with Grandma.

She clears the table, brings the pie, cuts big pieces, licks her fingers and wipes them on her apron. The juice has run out the little designs she made in the crust, turning the crust pink and rusty where it's toastier.

Suddenly everything stops. "What's the matter, John?" Grandma asks. She's hoping for a heart attack.

He pulls a gold ring out of his mouth and holds it up.

Grandma looks down at her hand. "Lord, think of that. You know, that ring used to be tight on me for years. Would you look at that."

I can't believe this won't upset Grandpa and get him started.

It seems like he's thinking really hard, and then says, *"Behold, I am against your magic bands with which you hunt the souls, and I will tear them from your arms; I will let the souls that you hunt go free like birds."*

"Wow." He always comes up with one that sort of fits.

Grandma pulls it away from him, runs in and rinses it off, and dries it on her apron. She puts it back on, shakes her head, then waves her apron at her face. I take my saucer and glass to the sink. "You eat the crust, Tina. That's the best part." I guess she's not that upset.

Grandpa's gone from shout to whisper, something about flinging us down on the ground. He's worse when he's whispery.

"You go ahead, Tina, and lie down or do your embroidery I got you started on. I'll pick up the kitchen." Embroidery. At least she's helping me get away from him, so I don't have to take this. Sometimes she's nice.

"Good pie," I say. She'd like to hug me. I go to my room and watch the window turn from dusk to dark. Pretty soon now.

"She's already asleep," I hear Grandma say. They go off to bed. They don't stay up late; they always have to beat the chickens getting up.

Now it's quiet, I can get out of here. I know exactly where to step so the linoleum won't snap, the boards won't groan.

Finally. I'm getting so cold. I see Gary coming.

"Hi."

"Hi."

"I thought tonight would never get here," I say.

"Yeah. Well, it's going to be better now. I'm taking you with me. Sooner than we thought. I've got everything in the pickup down the road. We can go to New Mexico. Wow. You're getting fat." He seems pleased enough about it. He kisses me like he loves me and then touches my belly like I'm a freak show.

"I can't go yet."

"Everything's ready."

"Yes," I say, "but I've got to solve this mystery." I can't even believe myself. "There's been a murder and I can solve it."

"What are you talking about?" Gary has a light little laugh that goes with any question. Sometimes it's really sexy. "Come on, New Mexico's going to be great."

"We can spend almost the whole night together this time," I say. "We can stay in that little house of the dead woman. I checked it out."

"I'd rather be in New Mexico."

"Have you ever been there?" He's never mentioned New Mexico to me. Let alone asked me if I have any big deal for New Mexico.

"No. That's one reason I picked it."

"Okay," I say. That seems a good reason. He kisses me again. "The baby moves now," I whisper when he sticks his hand under my shirt.

"Wow."

"I have to get some stuff."

"Let's not take any chances," he says. He doesn't look as cute when he's so nervous. "Let's leave. If you go back in there, the old man might wake up."

"I have to get something first."

"You don't need anything. We've got everything we need in the pickup."

"Wait here." I don't want to argue with him, so I just run through the cedars back into the yard and come back with what I need.

"What took you so long?"

"I only got two things." I follow him to the road. "Go slower. I'm pregnant."

"Ha ha." But he does get nice and helps me into his brother's pickup.

"Did he loan it to you," I ask, "or are we stealing it?"

"He gave it to me. Cause he says it'll be the only thing that'll make me happy pretty soon."

"Very funny."

"I gave him my rifle, my ten-speed, and my motor. So, he got something. You don't look so fat right now."

I'm so glad to be out of there, I can't even think for about fifty miles.

"I left them a note," I say. "I thought if I didn't they'd think I was kidnapped."

"Oh, great. You give them the license number, too?"

"I just said: Dear Grandma and Grandpa, I had to go. I'll call you up when the baby is born and tell you its name and which it is. Thanks for the pie and stuff. Your grand-daughter, Christina Rose."

"Not much of a note."

"There wasn't much time." We don't say anything again for a long time.

"What'd you bring with you?" he asks to help stay awake, while we're waiting to get on to the freeway.

"The list of baby names. And a jewel box." I finally open it, under those ugly freeway lights.

"You take that from your grandmother?"

"No. She took it from that old dead woman. She killed her. I'm saving her from prison."

"She didn't kill anybody. She just gets on your nerves." He thinks it's amusing. Wait until I tell him I plan to have a career as a detective. I'm not just going to wait on him.

I try to see which things in the jewel box show up with the dash lights of the truck. "This old bracelet is really beautiful," I say to Gary, holding it up to hang it on the rearview mirror.

"Emeralds," says Gary.

"They are. They're real."

"Sure."

I'm so sleepy, it takes me a while to realize, it's the stolen bracelet from the photographer, when my grandmother fell out the window. She must have pretended it was lost so she wouldn't have to give it back to the jeweler, but then felt so guilty or something, she gave it to Purla, or gave it to Purla because she was an Emblem and could handle it. They're probably not real, though. Or that jeweler would have had the cops in for sure. Maybe.

Gary wakes me up with the sky beginning to light up rose. "I'm cold."

"We'll get something to eat at this truck stop," he says. "You going to wear your jewels?"

"Leave me alone. I might throw up if this place looks icky."

"You still throwing up? It isn't quite morning yet. So if you hurry up and eat before it's morning you won't get morning sickness." He's trying to be helpful. I can see he doesn't want me to be a pain and drag everything down.

When we sit down and I look at the little kidney designs on the formica table, I suddenly realize something. "It was my grandfather! He took the bracelet and beat everybody up. He gave it to Purla. And he killed her. He did it all. The radio station. The six-inch blade, too! I better go back right now and save my grandmother."

"You still dreaming?" Gary grins. "Forget that crazy place, will you?"

"You're right. You want to hear some names?"

"Sure."

"Boys first or girls first?"

"Boys."

"Sherlock," I say, laughing.

"Hey, don't make fun of my kid," he says. And it makes me feel good.

"Did you ever hear of a woman having three breasts?" I ask.

"Oh, sure. Happens every day. Tails, too. Mermaids."

"I mean really."

"I knew a guy once that had webbed fingers. I think his toes were, too," he says. He's trying to be conversational. But sometimes Gary just doesn't get it.

I'm not going to tell him any of this stuff. I'll tell my grandchild.

"What are you so quiet about?" Gary asks.

"I'm thinking about what I'm going to tell my grand-children." He thinks that's funny. I'll let it go at that.

The Apocalypse
of Mary
the Unbeliever

MARY'S FATHER WAS A CARPENTER; work had been steady so Mary got a dollar a week for Woolworth's or the tin bank shaped like a mailbox. Mary was eleven years old and was developing breasts and suspicions, both of which she sought to conceal. "Mary," said her mother, "you move like a snail; finish those dishes." Mary smoothed over the flowers she had etched in the thick bacon grease of the frying pan and watched the water recede in angry gulps. Released from her trial at the sink, she sat in the bay window of the dining room, blowing on the window and making faces in the steam that wept down the windowpane. She looked through the teary, sagging faces she'd drawn in the window and saw her father's pickup come down the drive.

She stood in the utility room doorway and watched him set down his toolbox, take off his boots, step out of his carpenter's overalls with the wonderful pockets and tools, and finally remove his hard hat. Mary was intrigued that he could be so diminished in a matter of two minutes. A considerable man of canvas, leather, and metal willingly turned himself into a balding, narrow man, not much bigger than herself.

Her job was to hang his overalls on the nail, while he soaped his hands up to his elbows—lathering the ship on onc arm and the rose on the other—then splashed his face and bald head over the utility washtubs. She sat on the floor, vaguely feeling too big, but still too little to stop herself. She examined the nails in the gritty pockets: the punch, the tape, the hammer, the chalk line, and the flat pencil. Once she had taken the chalk line, hooking it to the antique chest and pulling its blue-chalked string across the carpet in the living room; she gave it a snap, and a fine blue line cut the room. But that had been two years ago and the last big trouble she had suffered. She hooked the overalls on the nail and waited for her father to take the old pink towel she held out to him. She regretted the water dripping off his nose and the tangle of hair and soap over his old tattoos. How'd he get so ugly, she thought, he never used to be.

"Why'd you get those tattoos?"

"So when I got a little girl, she'd have somethin' to pester me with when I was tired."

"Why really? Did you ever really think of me before I was born?"

"Nope."

"What did you think of when you had them made?"

"I thought it hurt like the devil."

"Do you believe in the devil?"

He stopped and looked at her so hard she backed up and tripped on his lunch bucket.

"Where'd you get all this talk about the devil?"

"*You* talked about it, you said so, when you . . ."

"Never mind. Never mind right now. Gotta talk this over with your momma."

"What?"

"Take my lunch pail and rinse the thermos."

Mary waited to hear about it over dinner. It was coming, she knew, when her father said, "New guy on the job."

"I hope," said her mother, "there's enough work for all of you to last through March."

"This guy," said her father, ignoring the threat of lay-offs, "is a preacher."

"Then why is he working as a carpenter?"

"That's what I said to him." Mary looked out the window to avoid her father's mashed potato mouth. "I said, 'Why's a preacher out poundin' nails?' He said it's just temporary 'til he gets his church goin'."

"He's a preacher without a church?"

"He remodeled his garage. Says he's made a nice church in the garage and he spent all their money on it. He's got five kids so he's gotta pound nails 'til he gets his church goin'."

"A church in a garage!" Mary hooted.

"Don't you never let me hear you talk that way again, Mary," her father said. "I s'pose you don't know they laid the Lord in a manger?"

"What?" asked her mother, looking as though she might tip the salad coated with Miracle Whip right into her dress. Mary silently watched them argue.

Her father looked down at his plate and conceded, "That's what the Rev said."

"The Rev?"

"Well, his name's Simon. He says just call him 'Rev.'"

"Oh, good. He should be a preacher or a carpenter, one or the other." Her mother lined up the salt and pepper shakers on either side of the napkin holder.

"S'pose you don't know what Joseph was? Joseph, the father of Jesus?"

"The Rev must have said that, too. What kind of church is it?" her mother snapped.

"Well, it's his own. He said he was trained to be a Presbyterian in the seminary, and when he got through, or was almost through, I guess, there was some things the Presbyterians had just plain wrong. And the main thing was on the devil and on the end time."

Mary, for the first time in her life, was interested in religion; for the first time in her life she was suspicious of it.

"Too much is happenin' is the devil," her father continued incoherently, "and the devil is showing hisself because of the end."

"God only knows about the devil or his end," said her mother.

Mary tittered, and her father repeated the words twice, washing out his wife's sarcasm and injecting them with new meanings. Mary was sure he would say it the next day to the Rev. She wished her brother were here. He would have laughed. She wrote to him in the Navy, asking him in every letter that if he ever thought about getting a tattoo to please talk to her first. She thought she would write to Tommy about this. He had written her back only two letters and signed both of them "Tom" as though he were someone else.

"Dear Tommy, Do you believe in the devil? I think we are getting into a church that's made out of a garage," she composed that night. "Be sure, if you are thinking of getting any tattoos that you talk to me about it first. Dad has met a preacher at the job. I love you. You are my brother. I am your sister and you should write to me. We are making cookies for you. Love. Mary."

That was Monday. By Wednesday Mary had forgotten and paid no attention to the sparks between her parents. She was changed. Katie, the girl next door, was fourteen and put up with Mary because of Tommy. Katie had played her "Heartbreak Hotel" record for Mary. Katie showed her a black and white picture of Elvis clipped from a magazine. Katie kissed it with her Fuchsia Midnight lipstick, and Mary hated how the picture was defiled with purple marks across his face. Mary memorized his name and that night wrote to

Elvis instead of her brother. She didn't know where to mail it, so she put a stamp on the envelope and buried it under the tree with the swing. Years later, after they were married, she would show him. Elvis Dear would swing her in the swing and then she would uncover the letter for him. He would smile at her, lip curled.

After school on Thursday, Mary emptied her mailbox bank and begged to go to town. To her surprise, her mother consented. She found the record and another, "I Want You, I Need You, I Love You." Best of all, she found a charm bracelet with his image, a little guitar, a dog, a shoe, and a record. She had enough left for a magazine filled with pictures of him. Her mother looked at her and said nothing.

Mary played the records and wore the charm bracelet. She looked at the pictures. She looked at herself in the mirror and thought she might change her mind about breasts.

Sunday morning she was told to dress up for church. She knew it wasn't going to be a real church, but she did her best in her dotted swiss dress her mother had made for her, flats, clutch bag, fuzzy nylon jacket, ribbon in her ponytail, and the Elvis Presley charm bracelet.

On the way to church, her father told them he'd done the Rev a good turn by letting the boss know that the preacher wasn't too bad a carpenter, and how you couldn't fault a preacher that worked for a livin'. They drove in the gray Northwest morning to the valley—land dotted with haphazard farms of people who made their living from jobs other than farming. When they got there, the church looked exactly like a garage. To her surprise, the preacher had kids around Mary's age; there was a girl named Barbara who was twelve, a boy named Edgar who was nine, and three that were little and sour-smelling. Mary didn't know what to say to kids who had a fake church in their garage. She stayed by their mother, fingering her bracelet, looking at the gravel, while the preacher's kids looked at her.

The preacher had wavy hair and a pointed face; he

was missing a part of a finger on his left hand. That means, thought Mary, he'd been carpentering a lot more than preachering. He took a ring of keys and unlocked the garage, beckoning everyone in. Mary looked around her and saw that it was just her family and theirs, plus two old ladies in veiled hats, and an old man in gray work clothes, gray cheeks, and a brown mouth.

Inside, Mary was disappointed. He had some real church pews all right, but they were crowded, and two were cut in half to make room for a big oil heater. On the platform was a pine lectern and a polished organ with a high, carved back. It looked like a fancy antique. The preacher didn't seem to know what to do next; everyone was as quiet as though the garage were a cathedral until the Rev flushed and said, "I'm going to take out that wall there and put in a stained-glass window." Mary looked at the garage windows and smiled. "Then I'm going to expand, soon's we have a bigger congregation, by knockin' out that wall and building thirty feet to the edge of the property. It'll have to be done by spring. That's when they'll start coming. That's when it'll be plain to everybody it's the End Time. I'll need your help, Brother George."

Mary's mother turned her back on them and gazed out the garage window at the thick, moist sky.

There was a picture of Jesus holding up two fingers. Mary looked at it, not thinking of Jesus, but thinking about Elvis and hearing him sing, "I Was the One."

"That's some organ you got there," said her father.

"Yep, we put every last cent we had in that organ. Now we're ready for the Lord to send us someone to play it."

"How long you had it?"

"Two months and haven't been able to hear a peep from it for the services." He looked at his flat-boned wife. "Most often a minister's wife carries that load." They looked at each other's mouths, but said nothing.

Mary's father was embarrassed. "I guess so. Guess I

should have been a preacher." The Rev scowled at him. "Because that's how Jennie courted me. She'd make me sit in her livin' room and listen to her recital pieces."

It was an old joke of her father's. Mary had always thought that her parents didn't look married. Not just because her mother was a little taller, much prettier; her bones, her hair, the shapes of her hands and the way she touched things made her look like someone else's wife, not the wife of a man with tattoos on his arms. Her father must have felt it, too. He liked to tell about Jennie playing the piano for him twenty years ago, excusing as a joke the discrepancy of all those years together.

"You play?" asked the preacher, looking at Jennie's back. It was the first time he had sounded anything like a preacher, like someone asking for something for the giver's own good.

"Oh, no," said Jennie, not acknowledging the request and barely turning toward him. "I forgot everything as soon as I married. I haven't touched the keys for twenty years."

"You'll play for us today. The gift to God's House is your hands." Mary moved closer to her mother. Jennie stood rigid against the absurdity of this unpleasant man touching her hands. Mary felt queasy; it sounded to her as if he wanted to cut off her mother's hands and keep them as relics in his garage.

"I can't. I don't even read music anymore."

"God will guide you. We will pray for God to guide your playing for His Glory."

"As long as God would be willing to take credit for what's off-key," she said to squelch him; but he took it for consent, although anyone could see that he didn't like that kind of tongue in a woman. He called her "Sister" and maneuvered her toward the organ, as she tried to keep her body from his hands. She sat down with a thump on the little claw-footed stool and the preacher kneaded her upper arms. Mary had never seen her mother look so helpless, her father so confused.

The preacher rushed off to a closet, threw a black robe over himself, and turned toward everyone, arms raised. Instead of a white minister's collar, the collar of a blue plaid flannel shirt poked up around his neck. He looks stupid, Mary thought; but she sat down, sorry that she could not sit by her mother. Her father was sitting on the other side, as close to his wife as he could manage. The preacher seemed changed. He began to fling his arms and draw out his words and phrases so long that none of his sentences made any sense to Mary. Everyone else was back by the oil heater so she couldn't look at them and see what they thought; but she could observe the wife, who was sitting directly in front of her preacher husband. We should call her, the preacher had said, "Sister Irene."

The Rev said, "Let us pray," and Mary heard the kids slipping out the back door. Sister Irene turned around, but directed her attention to Mary and hissed, "Close your eyes and fold your hands." It was as close as she could come to retrieving her own children.

Mary shut her eyes, unhooked her charm bracelet and held it. She couldn't do everything the woman told her. This was no real church. The preacher prayed to God to enter her mother, whom he called "Sister Genevieve" (although her name was Jennifer), and inspire her fingers to play the organ for His Glory. He made the request several times, and each time he said "Sister Genevieve," Mary opened her eyes to see her mother flinch. "Amen, brothers," said the preacher when he seemed to feel that he had gotten his message through. "Amen," and he slapped his hand with the missing finger against his open Bible.

"Let us turn now to hymn number 305; let us all rise and sing together." Mary wondered where he'd gotten the church things, the robe, the hymnals, the pews; she knew they weren't in stores, he must have stolen them from real churches. But, she thought, how could a preacher steal? She peeked behind to make sure that the three old people by the oil heater were standing before she stood up. "All right, Sister Genevieve, let's begin."

Jennie was paler than usual. "My name's Jennifer," she said and pulled out some stops, began to pump, and played the hymn with one hand.

The preacher didn't sing, so there wasn't much sound to fill in for the uncertain organ. He scowled and paged around in his Bible, "All four verses," he said when her mother tried to stop.

Then everyone sat down and the preacher talked about how whenever anything important happens God comes down and writes out a new name for it. He told how Sarai became Sarah and Abram, Abraham; how he was trained as a Presbyterian, but God gave him a new name for his true church, which was the True Church of God; and even, the preacher said, when someone seems like they're just a no-account woman good for makin' a hungry man a meal, God reaches down and changes her name to mark her, to tell her that he wants her to play His organ in His True Church, and that woman is Genevieve; and she's come just in time for the last church created to tell the final truth.

Mary had never seen anything like this preacher; grown-ups didn't get so embarrassed they had to make up whole dumb sermons just because they didn't know someone's name. Whenever Mary made a mistake, she liked to pretend she meant it all the time, like the day before when her mother called, "Please get the jam," and Mary had wandered to the pantry and taken the first thing she'd found. She brought a can of peas and set them absently on the counter. "Do you expect me to spread peas in a jelly-roll cake?" exclaimed her mother. "Where's your mind? I said, 'Please get me the jam!' It's in the refrigerator." "No," Mary had responded, "it was 'Peas, get them for Jen.'" "That's ridiculous. I've never said anything like that. I wouldn't refer to myself by name. You can see I need the jam to roll this cake." "I'll get you the jam," Mary said, "but next time you should say what you want." "Why do you do these things, Mary? Once you get yourself into something, you can't let yourself out." Mary got the homemade jam out of the refrigerator and left the room as her mother said, "A little embarrassment doesn't have to be painted over with a lie."

The preacher was going on now about how the devil was getting into everything, and she could tell that her father liked this part. It was about Communists and sex and movie pictures and showing it was Time. Mary drifted off, hearing her records at home, deciding what dress she would be wearing when she was a movie star and Elvis came to meet her. She would be in a movie with a long, green velvet dress, and Elvis would come to watch her say her part and would weep just a little from her scene. Her name would be Marissa...but suddenly Mary felt that something was wrong. She wasn't going to do anything like this preacher; she wasn't going to be a movie star. She'd never change her name; Elvis would just have to call her Mary. Elvis would come to her because she was a famous archaeologist, and he would say, "Mary, I know this island where there's a buried castle. I need you so we can dig it up. The walls are all carved and say mysterious things only you can figure out. It's filled with treasure; you can wear all the jewels." Mary and Elvis stepped onto the lush island just as her mother began to pump the organ again.

Mary didn't know what page she was supposed to be singing, but then she saw that Sister Irene was passing a basket for money. The Rev was making a big plea for money, and Mary thought that he was getting carried away for nothing. Sister Irene held the basket before her father and he put in ten dollars. She came over and held the basket toward Mary, who opened her clutch purse and saw that she had only two pennies and the dollar her father had given her the day before. Nothing in between. Why couldn't that ten dollars be for all of them, she thought, I'm a kid. She was going to put in the pennies when the wadded dollar sprang out of her purse. Sister Irene scooped up the dollar and put it in the basket. Mary fought back tears; it would be another whole week before she could get "Don't Be Cruel." Her mother was experimenting with two hands, but God didn't seem to have his hand in it. Sister Irene came back to her pew, sat down, and the organ wheezed and stopped. Mary saw Sister Irene bundle up the money and stick it inside her dress.

There was more praying, another whole sermon about the Catholics, the Jews, and the final True Church of God, another four-verse hymn, and two more prayers. Through it all Mary was so distracted she was barely able to reach the place on the jungly island where Elvis was pointing out to her the turrets of the medieval castle protruding through the trees.

Outside, at last, Mary realized that the True Church had retained the odor of a garage, and she breathed the damp air gratefully.

The kids—she had forgotten about them—came toward her like gangly-legged birds. Her father said, "You run play with the kids. We'll call you when we're ready." Barbara pulled her hand and Edgar pushed at her back, and they ran her around to the other side of the house where they could not be seen.

"Do you always dress like that?" asked Barbara. She was in old pedal pushers.

"No, I usually wear Jantzen sweaters and tight skirts," Mary lied, conveniently appropriating Katie's wardrobe, "but this is for your dad's church."

"I can't stand church," said Barbara.

"Neither can I," Mary said. "Why did your dad make it?"

"I don't know and I don't care."

"I know some kissing games we can play," said Edgar and he pounced on Mary and threw her to the ground. She struggled free, picked up her purse with one hand and held her braceleted wrist with the other. She'd never seen such awful children.

"Go away, Edgar," said Barbara, tossing her thumb

over her shoulder like a truck driver. "Let me see that bracelet." Mary held her arm out stiffly to the side.

"Let me see that purse," said Edgar. Mary held it out, knowing there was nothing left but two pennies and a hanky printed with roses that her grandmother had told her to keep at all times in her purse. Nevertheless, she kept one hand on it, as Edgar tried the catch and rummaged in it. Her arms were extended, one to each side, as Edgar and Barbara picked at her possessions.

"Elvis Presley! My dad won't let me have anything to do with him. Wait'll he finds out! Do you have any of his records?"

"Two."

Barbara smiled. "He'll make you break them in the garage." She doesn't even call it a church, thought Mary. "And, he'll take this bracelet, too, and make you throw it in the garbage. Then I'll get it."

"How could you have it if he wouldn't let me have it?" Mary felt herself tumbling into the terrible logic of Barbara's world.

"I'll hide it. Only wear it to school. He won't know about it."

"He won't know that I have it."

"Yes. I'm tellin' him just as soon as you go." They held the moment, and then Barbara continued, "Unless you let me wear it now. Just while you're here. It's only fair. He keeps me from havin' all the stuff you do. I bet you have a room all to yourself, don't you?"

"Yes."

"Well, you get this bracelet every day. Let me wear it for this time and I won't tell."

"We're never coming back."

"Yes, you are. Your dad'll make you." How did she know so much? "So I'll help you. I'll make sure he doesn't find out. Just let me wear it for now."

Mary didn't like the argument, but thought that if she let Barbara wear it just this little while, she would keep

Edgar away from her. He was sitting on the lumpy grass watching. "Okay." She felt a twinge as she unhooked the bracelet and placed it around the other girl's arm. They compared their schools and, when Edgar rolled on the lawn aiming to look up Mary's dress, Barbara kicked him several times in the chest and took Mary to the other side of the large yard that still looked more like pasture than lawn.

Mary saw the adults come out of the house and her mother motion for her. "Give me my bracelet. I have to go."

"Be careful," Barbara whined. "Do you want my dad to notice? You get in the car and roll down the window and act normal. Then, just at the last second before you drive off, I'll reach in the window like I'm touching you good-bye. I'll give it to you then, so no one will see." Barbara gave her a little push toward the adults.

Mary got in the car, rolled down the window, and didn't stop watching Barbara. "Okay. Now," said Mary.

"Wait," she whispered and motioned with her hand toward the preacher.

"*Now*," pleaded Mary as her father started the car. Barbara bolted around the house as Mary's father pulled out. She waved to Mary from the edge of the yard, grinning. Mary couldn't tell her parents because she felt stupid and because she could feel what was welling up between the grown-ups.

Finally, her mother said, "Genevieve. Organ-playing. Giving those people our money." Mary remembered her dollar and felt outsmarted by all of them. "True Church of God, my foot. I'm not going back ever to the Reverend Simon's True Church."

"Not so fast now, Jennie. We've got to realize there's not much time left."

"I'm not going back to that True Church of God!"

Mary suddenly realized she might never see her bracelet again and yelled, "*I'm* going back to that True Church of the Garage!"

Her mother looked surprised. Her father thumped the

steering wheel and said, "Now that's a sign. Just like that rainbow up ahead." Jennie said nothing more but let her tears soak the tips of her white gloves. Mary wondered why all this church stuff made her so sick and thought, As soon as I get my bracelet I'm going to tell them what I think. If I tell them now, I'll never get my bracelet back from that ugly old Barbara.

Her father came home on Tuesday and paced the kitchen. "There's going to be a layoff. I didn't think there'd be any."

"Last man hired, first one fired," her mother sang.

"Well." He didn't go on. He poured some Hi-C and drank it like he was pretending it was whiskey. "Well. Not this time. The boss said he just can't fire a man who's got five kids when we've only got one, and we're in pretty good shape. And he just can't fire a preacher, he says, who gets out and works for a livin', not like most."

"He's not a real preacher!" Jennie screamed and knocked the rice onto the floor. Then she slipped on the hot, steaming mess and as she fell she caught a green mixing bowl and cut her hand so badly that Mary's father said, "You'll have to be sewed up. Have to get you downtown. Hurry!"

"No! Not until I change my dress! I can't go anywhere with rice stuck to my dress."

Mary was frightened; her stomach felt like someone was digging a grave inside it. But she was curious too, to see her mother screaming and irrational. There wasn't nearly as much rice as blood on her dress.

"Mary!" her father yelled, "Clean this up while I help your mother change her dress."

"I can't. There's blood in it."

"Leave it. Leave it," her mother said. "It's a sign of the End Times."

"You're just getting dramatic, Jennie. Mary, I'll whip your butt."

Mary obeyed, mostly because she thought it was the

first time he sounded like himself since the Rev had come on the job.

"We can't spend money on the doctor now," her mother sobbed.

"My job lasts two more weeks. I'll find another."

"Not in November."

Mary watched the red spot grow on the apron wrapped around her mother's hand until it was all soaked by the time they got to town. She watched the doctor stitch her mother's flesh. Now two dresses were ruined with blood. The doctor clucked at her and told her to look out the window. It was dark; there was nothing to see. When Mary heard the doctor tell her mother to keep her hand out of water for a while, she knew what it meant for her. That damn preacher, she thought, and was pleased that the first time she swore it was aimed right at the True Church of the Garage.

"Well, at least..." Mary tried to comfort her mother after she was in bed and still shivery, "at least you won't have to be God's organ-player for a while."

Jennie's shivering stopped. "Mary, why did you say you want to go back there?"

"Because," and Mary hesitated. She felt as though she could be blamed for everything and her whole future on the island as an archaeologist with Elvis Presley would be lost. "Because most people go to church, don't they?"

Jennie shut her eyes.

On Friday Mary came home from school ready to play her two records, but found a note on the refrigerator. "Mary. Be back soon. Stay home. Love, Mom." The note was written with the wrong hand because the right was bandaged. It made it look like her mother was crazy. Mary looked for something to put on a slice of bread and ended up using it to blot her tears of self-pity. She knew it was worse than she could imagine. And it was.

When her mother came home she took a long time to tell her that her father was in the hospital. "There was a terrible, freak accident on the job," and she finally admitted, "He lost his hand."

"The preacher did it," Mary wailed.

"Here. The doctor wants you to take this. Then you can stay home from school tomorrow and we'll go see him."

"Tomorrow's Saturday. And I don't want any pill. He's not going to get my hand or my bracelet either."

"The doctor was afraid of this. If you don't take it, he'll come over and give you a shot."

Mary took the pill, minutely chewing its bitterness, making sure nothing was hidden inside it, and washed it down with Hi-C.

She fell asleep as Elvis and she pulled back the vines from a great, aged door. They pushed it open, and to make sure it was safe, he sang into the darkness, "Anyway You Wa-a-a-Hant Me," his voice filling the mysterious, cavernous rooms, heaped with treasures.

The next day Mary stood in the hospital room, looking at the old man in the next bed, not at her father. Jennie arranged her husband's pillows, the flowers, the water glass and pitcher, pretending to keep house around the bed.

They looked up when the Rev appeared in the doorway, intoning, "Have no concern. He will return and restore us all." He touched Mary's face with the hand that missed a finger, reached out for Jennie's bandaged paw, and kept his eyes on the place where there was nothing below George's sailing ship. "Don't have any concern. Let us pray together and thank the Lord. It's a blessed sign from God that He wants Brother George to spend all his time doin' His work and that the End is close."

Mary just knew that either she was never going to get that bracelet back, or she was going to end up caught in that True Church of the Garage and Jesus was going to spend his own sweet time coming back. And she fell against her mother, like a little child, though only half a head shorter: "Momma, Barbara took my bracelet and kept it."

Intestate and Without Issue

"**I**NTESTATE AND WITHOUT ISSUE." MAR-
della studies the paper up close to her eyes. "Hmm? Nonnie,
you know you're welcome to the use of my carnival glass
punch set. Only be careful. They're worth a pretty penny
now. Gladys only give them to me cause they shamed her.
Now she covets them."

"What's that, Mardella?" The women look like clab-
bered milk in the bright yellow kitchen.

"That's what this lawyer paper says about Vernon. Intestate and without issue." She hesitates to hand over the
document.

"I know all about it," Nonnie says, running her finger
along the heavy pressed glass of the punch bowl. "I've seen
it. Means he didn't have kids."

"Means he didn't have a will."

"Means Mr. Carter's gotta come up with somebody to
give Vernon's inheritance to." Nonnie grins, a flash across
her pale, narrow face.

"Don't amount to a hill a beans." Mardella shrugs her
flesh and sits down at the kitchen table.

"Might be suprised." Nonnie raises her eyebrows to top her smile.

"Well, Nonnie, the old Wilson place is a dreadful sight, but I spose someone could patch it up and set it to rights, at the least, keep it from rottin out more'n it has."

"You could probly find you some more carnival glass in that house, Mardella."

"More'n that. If whoever ends up with that old place can get possession fore the kids break in and spoil it."

"And haul it away, sellin it to you, Mardella, spoon by spoon."

"Ah, you know my weakness for a fancy dish. Though Lord knows I don't put up no stores against tomorrow." Mardella lays down the paper and sets her palms up on the table like little saucers.

"I know your weakness for inheritin." Nonnie leans a little toward Mardella, her long hands pressed on the table-cloth, like fans of forks and knives at a picnic. "You sure give to old Miss Puckett. Pies, cool cloths to her head, even changin her didies when she was down bad, all so she'd write you in. Same with Uncle Bill, goin over an puttin fresh dressins on those stinkin legs ever night. Feedin him like a baby. Same with your second husband, for that matter."

"Lord, Nonnie, I dearly loved my Ben, rest his soul. What's got into you?" She gets up. "You wanna help me wrap up the punch set or you wanna make me feel lonesome?"

"Can't say you didn't marry Ben without him already bein a sickly man. I want you to own up for once."

"Lord ha'mercy. I could say this: I could say I've had me two husbands, two more'n you'll ever have."

"Well, Mardella, this here's goin to suprise you. Sure is." Nonnie takes a walk around the kitchen. "When Vernon and me went off that time..." She gazes out into the back-yard. "We got married." She looks into the sink and whispers. "One place or nother there's a marriage license and I got that inheritance comin. After I see Mr. Carter again," she looks straight at Mardella, "you can come on over to admire my carnival glass, my cut glass, my RS Prussia china. I know, well as you, what's in that house. It's mine. My house."

"You think I believe you? You was never married, Nonnie. To Vern nor to nobody else. If you was, you'da carried on all up'n down this valley."

"All you know, missy. I couldn't marry no one so long as Daddy was alive. So Vern'n me kept it secret."

"Then, if that's so, swear on this Bible'n tell me why didn't you set up house with Vern after your daddy was passed on?" The crocheted, cross bookmark slips from the Bible and Mardella coaxes it back in.

"Didn't want to no more." Nonnie rests her eyes in the bowls of her hands, her arms thin stems to the tablecloth.

"You're only makin this up to spite me."

"Spite you?" Her arms fold themselves.

"You know good'n well I got plans for that Wilson place. I'm gonna fix it up for Boo and James Everett," she confides.

"You're always doin for somebody."

"That's the way I am." Mardella slips the lawyer's photocopy in with the cross.

"Well, sorry to disappoint you, Mardella, in your charitable deed. That Wilson place is mine. I'm the Missus. And as rightful owner, I will swear on a stack of Bibles to prove it so." She places both hands on Mardella's Bible.

"Honey, you know you're not. You've jest gone soft in the head cause all your prospects is in their graves. Your daddy's been gone five years." Mardella pulls her Bible out from under Nonnie's hands, their four hands together for a moment like a family of bristly little pigs, until she puts the book on the windowsill next to the jade plant. "You had plenty time to make it known, if you was married."

Nonnie whispers, "He's been gone nine years. Nine, goin on ten, Daddy's been gone."

"Nine. No."

"Yes ma'm. Goin on ten." They look into each other's

faces, searching for the years. "It'll be ten." They look past each other, erasing what they saw.

"Lord. Well, hold this chair steady while I climb up to reach them punch cups. How many you gonna need?" Mardella pulls a chair close to the cupboard.

"All eleven of them. Gladys is gonna come, too."

"One's chipped," Mardella says as she hoists herself onto the chair.

"I know. Has been for a long time. We'll keep it in the kitchen in case Boo comes on down." Nonnie clamps her hands on the chair back.

"She's too far gone to come gallavantin. Already past her due date."

"That's what I figure. But I like to have the cup in case."

"Boo's my baby. If she comes on down, I'll rinsh my own cup out'n use the chipped one myself." She hands cups to Nonnie, one by one.

"Mardella, you're always doin for others." Nonnie places them gently in the dish drainer.

"I try. So, how come you never to move in with Vernon? You're gonna have to cook up some tall story if you're tryin to get poor little Boo's house out from under her. Lord, Nonnie, you know James Everett can't work no more," Mardella says from the height of the chair.

"Never could, far as I know."

"And you know Boo's expectin her third."

"Yes, I know. You got all those grandchildren now, Mardella. You're gettin old." She looks up critically at Mardella, appraising her as though she were the inside of a musty closet.

"Same age as you. As young as you."

"You're six months older. And six months bigger."

"Hold that chair still. You've said that since we was girls. You'd think you'd get tired of your meanness one of these days."

"I didn't make it up. Matter of fact, it was Vern who first said it."

"Now you know that's not true. Vernon always took a shine to me. Remember the time he said he liked my dress? You turned round, went home like a wet hen. Looks like we're gonna have to wash out these cups. When's the last time we used them?"

"When Addie had that Tupperware party."

"Been awhile. This punch set's too fine for things like that. Addie never could set a table. Nonnie, I do believe your hair's thinnin."

"Get down now. Hold on to my hand."

"You can't go traipsin around town claimin you was married to Vernon, bless him." She eases down from the chair and flicks a dishcloth across its seat. "Everone knows you always made a fool of yourself over Vernon. If you go off tellin trash as this on yourself, the County will come and cart you off."

"You can't stand it cause you know it's true. Sometimes I was bustin to tell you, Mardella, but I didn't want it spread all over the valley. I wouldn't of hurt Daddy for the world."

"Then what'd you get married for? I'm not sayin you did, understand. But if. Why would you take a chance on your little daddy findin out?" She makes a sink of suds as she makes her case.

"I tell you, Mardella, I may not think my name's nailed up all over Heaven the way you do, but I got me a spot saved there. And I tell you, girl, whenever Vern used to look on me, I thought I would melt." Nonnie watches the cups rock and sink into the hot water. "Daddy was little, but he was powerful."

"You always did look like you was comin into heat round Vern, as I recall it. You mean you went to the trouble of gettin married secret?" Mardella snorts.

"Yes, ma'm," Nonnie whispers. "I knowed that boy was gonna have me, and I knowed I was no sinner. So I fixed it with the Lord. Then, oh my, Vern did not disappoint. Never did."

"Hmm. You think you fix hornswaggles with the Lord?

If you talk like that, you won't even go to Heaven. You'd melt the Pearly Gates, you're so hot." Mardella laughs. "And if you was so sweet on Vernon, God rest his soul, answer my question: how come didn't you move on over with him, or him with you, after your daddy, bless his old soul, was gone?"

"Well, if you gotta know, Mardella. I come to be used to things the way they was."

"And the fire went out?" She rinses cups, handing them into Nonnie's dish towel.

"Vernon, like us all, woke one day and his good looks had come up missin. But, honey, his fire never went out." Nonnie carries cups to the table.

"Don't I know it."

"What?" She snatches at a cup and Mardella's sigh.

Mardella lays newspapers on the table. "You want the pedestal with the bowl?"

"Course. That's what makes it so pretty."

"Ever last one of them comin to your party knows perfectly well that's my punch set."

"We all know it's your punch set, Mardella. Gladys told Addie, though, it's really hers, on loan to you, cause you were so good to her Uncle Bill fore he passed on."

"That woman's got another think comin." She rattles paper around a cup. "After she married that stranger and her mother-in-law come from Baltimore to stay with her, she give up the whole punch set to me. Gladys said, 'Why I can't abide this old garish punch set on my sideboard.' Seems she got that idea from Baltimore. Though she soon found out she shoulda been shut of her mother-in-law long fore that woman finally packed all her hats and highheels back to Baltimore."

"I always think no good will come from a mother-in-law who's younger than the bride." Nonnie wads paper and lays the clumsy ball on the table.

"That's the truth. Poor Gladys. I heard, you know I'm not one to tell tales, but I heard that they had a fight over

Vernon, bless his soul, who had took to settin on their veranda ever evenin. But I'm not one to cast a shadow on the tomb."

"Oh, Mardella, you know, myself, and everone in town knows, he got Gladys' mother-in-law p.g. That's how come that mother-in-law to disappear."

"Did she ever have that baby, I wonder?" She looks at the papers Nonnie hands her, as though she might read about it in the dried-up news.

"Spose so. Well, bein from Baltimore she might not. Shall I ask Gladys?"

"Nonnie. Don't you dare."

"You expect me to try to lose my own inheritance to some stranger in Baltimore? You forget, Mardella, I'm coming into some propity. Soon's I get me some legal advice. Some papers. Sure don't want Gladys to get wind of this. If she don't know yet."

"My lips is seals. Darlin, I sure do hate to tell you this. But that Wilson place is comin to me."

"You already told me, Mardella. But you didn't have no way of knowin that I was married to Vern nor that I'm ready to tell it now. It's mine. Course I don't know how you could of collected anyway. You couldn't of talked your way into his will cause he was intestate. That the word?" She leans over to pluck the sheet sticking out from the Bible.

"Yes, Nonnie, intestate. But the lawyer paper says intestate and without issue. I'm ready now to say he was not, no sirree, not without issue."

"I spose you got a kid of his, hid down in the cellar," she titters.

"Nope. She's right out in the open," Mardella says softly.
"What?"

"Where do you think I got my Boo?"

"You lie like a rug, Mardella."

"I'm not lyin," she gasps. "Do you think I'd worry Boo with this old mess if it wasn't to bring her a blessin?"

"I know you'd never harm a hair of your baby. I know.

Mardella, what makes you think you can get away with sayin all of a sudden she's got a new daddy she had all along? Who you spect would believe that?"

"Can or not, as they choose. I can prove it."

"Devil get you for lyin same as stealin."

"If Vern had knowed James Everett was goin to knife him right there in the Red Rooster, he'd a made certain he wouldn't a gone to his Maker intestate."

"James Everett, the way you got it planned, stands to inherit from the man he murdered. That's about the ugliest thing I've ever heard, Mardella."

"Can't say murder. Seventeen witnesses. Self-defense. Don't you never call Boo's husband a murderer."

"Boo and James Everett don't even hardly speak to one another. And her about to give birth." Nonnie pats her neck.

"He'll come round when the baby's born."

"Good God Amighty, Mardella, don't you know what it was James Everett stabbed Vern over in the first place? Tomi says James Everett slammed Vernon up against the jukebox and played all heck with the record that was on at the time. No one has ever got tired of Hank Williams, all these years, have they? So Tomi got Lester to open up that jukebox and give her the record as a keepsake. She says those big old scratches on the record put her in mind of Vern."

"You hush your mouth. Bless his soul. Tomi's only a half-witted girl. Workin in that old bar." Mardella swats at the thought.

"She saved the record. 'Your Cheatin Heart.' She showed it to me. Maybe that throwback thinks she's got somethin to inherit. She says she was thick with Vern. You think Lester will replace that song or put in another Willie Nelson?"

"Lord, Nonnie, you don't care nothin for Vernon's memory."

"Tomi was mighty distressed over James Everett layin into Vern anyway. He kept comin in, claimin Boo was hatchin Vernon's baby. That's what they come to fight over."

One of the wadded packages hits the floor with a muffled crunch. "Look what you made me do! Made me drop this cup. Could hear it break through the paper. I hope it was the chipped one. Look." Mardella pulls back the paper like bandages from a wound. "It's all broke to pieces. Here. Help me unwrap these. See if it was the chipped one. If it wasn't, I don't know how we'll get by." She sits down to think. "I'll drink out of the chipped one at your party, then if Boo comes in to town anyway, I'll jest rinsh it out and let her use it. If we're lucky Gladys or nobody won't notice we're down to ten."

"You tellin the truth about Boo? About Vernon bein her real daddy?"

"You think I could make it up? You do. Cause you concocted that story about bein secretly married to Vernon, bless him."

"Shoot, Mardella, here's the chipped one. I guess you're down to ten and one of them is a chipped one. Nothin lasts forever."

"You best be thinkin how you're goin to find me another one, Nonnie. Can't order it from the catalogue. Can't find it at K Mart. Can't wish it here."

"Don't get all teary-eyed. When I get that Wilson place, I've got a mind to make you a present of a china sugar bowl. Even the lid's perfect. It says Limoges on the bottom. Pale rose sprays. Gold trimmed. Not a craze. Least that's how I remember."

"Boo's gonna have that Wilson place and don't you forget it." Mardella lifts the punch bowl from its glass stand and turns the stand upside down. "See, if you don't wanna use it as the base, you can use the bowl plain, then you can stick flowers in this part and you got a matchin purple carnival vase."

"Mardella. You must be the last one in the valley to hear what James Everett got so worked up over with Vernon."

"You got no respect for the dead. You're jest like your daddy."

"My daddy is one of the dead and you better get some respect."

"You got me all beside myself, Nonnie. I can't think straight. I don't dare let this punch bowl outa my sight. This is a Northwood. That's what this N inside the little circle stands for on the bottom."

"I know. I know. Peacock at the Fountain pattern."

"When's that old party of yours anyway?"

"In three days. You know well as I do."

"Three days. I'll bring the dishes over tomorrow then. God willin. There's plenty time."

"Mardella. If you run out sayin Vern was Boo's daddy, then you give her a sight more trouble than she needs. If she's carryin Vern's baby. You may as well hang a scythe over that baby's head. It won't have a chance."

"You can jest leave, go on home. You can go to Goligarthee. Your ugly talk. I'll pray for your soul all night long, but I won't look at your ugly face no more today."

"Can't leave now. Someone's knockin at the door. Maybe you should talk to Boo. I heard she's been in to see Mr. Carter herself. Who knows what James Everett'll do then."

"Answer the door. You got any manners left?"

"Wipe your eyes. It's your door. Not mine. But I'll get it." Nonnie opens the back door. "Mmm. Oh, honey! Mardella, look who's here at the door. We got little Beverly Kay come to visit. Hey, Sweetheart, you're a pretty sight."

"I know, pretty as a bug's ear. You told me before." Beverly Kay prances in and examines the papers and glassware. "Hey. Guess what!"

"What, honey? You want some bread and jam? I got some milk here," says Mardella.

"Ick. I don't drink milk. You got any Coke?" Beverly Kay opens the refrigerator.

"You look more like Addie ever day. Don't she, Nonnie?"

"Sure does. You sure look like your momma."

"Momma look like a bug to you?" Beverly Kay rests her

buckle shoe on the crisper drawer, her hair strings over the covered dishes as she leans into the refrigerator, removing a bowl.

"What? You want this gravy? You know, baby, you can have whatever your heart desires, but I can't imagine what you want with gravy. Maybe I can heat it up and put it over these potatoes for you," Nonnie offers.

"No!" Beverly Kay shoves the bowl back in. "I thought it was puddin. We have puddin I make myself, just shake it up with milk. Guess what! We're gonna be rich. I heared Momma talkin on the phone again to the lawyer. She says I can't tell no one. I come to tell you, though. Cause she says soon as it's out, she won't be goin to Nonnie's old party, that's one thing for sure. Can I have this mushmelon, please?"

"What do you mean, honey?" Nonnie quickly gets a knife and splits the melon.

"Nonnie, don't ask the child to talk, not if her momma told her to keep a secret." Mardella spoons out the seeds.

"I'll keep her secret with her, you know that." Nonnie squats down close, "Beverly Kay, darlin, your momma already said she's for sure comin. I know for a fact what she's wearin. I helped her pin up the hem myself."

"That pink thing? Ick. She looks like a hollyhock in that old thing and I told her so too."

"Well, I should think a hollyhock is real dainty," frowns Mardella.

"Ick. You let them grow back of your house. But we pulled ours all up. I don't care for that melon now, thank you kindly anyway. You sliced it funny. I think I'll just have a little bread and butter, not to put you out none."

"You sure you want this bread, honey? Don't want to make you sick to your stomach come dinnertime."

"Let the girl talk a minute. I mean breathe. Bread and butter, honey pie?"

Beverly Kay opens the refrigerator again. "We just found

out we're goin to be rich. How come you always got leftovers, but you never got any beginnins? My momma talked to the lawyer on the phone. And he says looks like she's about as airtight as need be to get that old propity."

"What? You're just a baby, honey. You don't know what you're talkin about." Mardella pats the girl's head and guides her from the refrigerator.

"I do so. I guess you're just all out of soda." She ducks from under Mardella's meddling with her hair. "I know James Everett stabbed Mr. Vernon to death in three places, once in the eye, Mr. Vernon died right there, jerkin in his blood all over, and left all his gold and house to my momma and me." She pulls a chair up to the cupboard and asks, "Where's your cake sparkles at?"

"There's no will, honey. You'll learn about these things when you get big. Vern went to Heaven intestate and without issue. And you're too young to know what that means." Nonnie hands Beverly Kay the little bottles of cake decorations and helps her off the chair.

"I am not. I know it means they're lookin for who to give all the gold and the propity to." She opens the red glittery sugar and shakes it over her bread and butter.

"There's no gold, child. Thou shalt not covet." Mardella stands over her, watching her add green glitter.

"There might be gold. Anyway, we get it all. Where are those little silver beebees?"

"The silver ones is only for wedding cakes, doll baby, or for showers. Vern never had nothin to do with Addie. Never," Nonnie declares.

"Ssh. Don't speak so in front of the child. Sugar, your momma, is she sayin that Mr. Vernon was..."

"Mr. Vernon and my Papaw."

"What? Now I won't hear such things. I've covered my ears up," Nonnie cries and finds the bottle of silver shot high in the cupboard.

"Can I have another bread and butter to take to Thomas?"

"You sure can, doll baby. You always think of your brother Thomas. When you get to Heaven you'll get a crown for sure." Mardella hands her another slice of buttered bread, like her ticket to cash in at the Gate.

"I might buy me a crown of my own. Soon's we get that propity."

"What makes your momma so positive?" Nonnie smirks.

"Cause she took Gran's Bible to the lawyer. Before Papaw and Mr. Vernon went off to fight they wrote in Gran's Bible that when one died the other got his propity, forever and ever. And Papaw says he remembers the whole thing, clear as day." Beverly Kay licks the tablecloth.

"That's not so."

"Yes it is." Beverly Kay sprinkles the sugared bread with red, green, and gold. "And the lawyer told my Momma there's five women with bright red faces right now." She holds up her moist, glittered hand.

"What?"

"Five women been sayin they kissed and hugged Mr. Vernon so they could get his propity. They all already been to see the lawyer. I got to put lots of these little chocolate sprinkles on; Thomas calls 'em rat pats. He likes 'em best."

"You run along home, sugar. You take the bread to Thomas."

"Well. When we're rich, Momma says we're gonna throw a party for spite. You all can come. Papaw says we can do whatever we want, he's gonna set right where he is."

"Well, you better go along now, Beverly Kay. We got us a busy day here."

"Bye bye," Beverly Kay licks the corner of her mouth.

"Bye, honey pot." Nonnie aims her toward the door.

"Thank you for the bread and butter. You got any more colors? Thomas doesn't like it sparin, he likes it heaped."

"You go on, now. I believe you got it all. Bye now."

Nonnie shuts the door and watches out the window. "Mmm."

"Lord." Mardella sits down, leans toward the window

and retrieves the paper from the Bible. She unfolds it, folds it again, and uses it to scrape the colored sugar on the tablecloth into little piles. Nonnie brings out the broom, sugar crunching on the linoleum.

"I just feel like I been run over by lightnin."

"Lord God ha'mercy."

"You know, Mardella, honey, I was just a pullin your leg about that marriage license. I never had no use for gettin married and never will. You always knowed that."

"I knowed it." Mardella squeezes Nonnie's hand. "Why in God's green world do you think I made up that whopper about Boo? You know I never strayed."

"Sure do. Not anymore than Boo herself would ever stray."

"I should say."

"Though with Boo, I'd say James Everett gives her plenty good reason."

"You mean to tell me, Nonnie, that James Everett accused my baby of sin right there in front of all those fools at the Red Rooster?"

"Well, now, I got that from Tomi. She says so."

"I'll split open his gullet."

"No. I guess you won't do nothin." They pull their chairs close to each other and sit down.

"James Everett will never get Boo out of that old mobile home and into her own place with room enough for those babies. How I've tried ever way I know to help them."

"Don't I know it. Least ways, with Addie thinkin she's goin to own the whole east side of town now, what with that poor old Wilson place, we won't have to worry about cups enough to go around. Boo can jest come ahead."

"Yes. Let's get this bowl and pedestal wrapped. I'll get out some towels to put around them."

"You gonna let me use them, for sure, Mardella? You don't mind?"

"What put that in your head? What's mine is yours. I spent my whole life givin, I'm not gonna stop now."

"We'll never tell no one, will we?"

"I don't even know what you're talkin about, Nonnie."

"We won't tell. If one tells, then the other would have to. That wouldn't do."

"Sounds like cuttin off your nose to spite your face."

"Course, there's nothin to tell really. I meant it all as a little joke. I was funnin you."

"Me, too. Me, too."

"But we'll make a pact anyway, Mardella."

"I got jest the thing. We'll need a real secret to keep between us. Not these old made-up stories, Nonnie."

"Leastways not a bit of truth to mine."

"Not to mine neither. Get me a screwdriver out of that bottom drawer by the stove."

"What you want with a screwdriver?"

"We're gonna make a secret pact."

"Draw blood with the thing?"

"Don't be a fool. We're goin in through the back of the Wilson place. I know how. Sheriff Puckett thinks he's got it tight as a drum to keep those kids from messin around in there."

"What's got into you?"

"I'm goin to have my Limoges sugar bowl. The one you promised to me. What're you goin to have, Nonnie?"

"I think Vern wanted me to have that flow-blue platter."

"They won't be missed. Addie's never knowed a nice thing when she looked right at it."

"We may as well get those silver teaspoons. They've been black as sin for years."

"You think we could get holda that china-headed doll?"

"Don't see why not. Mardella, I wasn't goin to tell you this, but I'm sure there's three good pieces of carnival glass over there. Even an Acorn Burrs pattern fluted bowl."

"Vern, bless his heart, never paid them a bit of attention."

"After old Mrs. Wilson died, no one ever laid a dust rag to none of it."

"I know this, Nonnie. If Vern hadn't of died so sudden, so intestate, he'd have seen to it hisself that we got what we cared for."

"I know. And we'll never tell no one. Addie can have the old house. It will cost more in soap powders and glass panes than the thing's worth."

"Lord a mercy, that's the truth. She'll never get to it, neither. Beverly Kay's hair's always a rat's nest."

"I never felt so close to you before, darlin. It makes me feel like we're doin the right thing."

"We're doin the right thing by Vernon. He just wishes it was more. He's up in Heaven sayin, 'Lord God, how is it a man gets caught intestate?'"

Foxglove

"**N**O," I HAD SAID.

"Well, little Catie, if you don't have a book of your very own, you'd better just come up to my back porch and I'll see that your name is inscribed on the flyleaf of a fine book. I have one waiting for you."

"No," I had repeated inaudibly. I remember myself, long ago, as a tight little bud of a child.

The sleeve of his wool jacket, woven in a pattern that imitated feathers, scratched against my cheek. I think I remember that even then John made me feel wary, the scent of him; he smelled like a man made of wool and feathers. My father smelled like gasoline. If only I had discovered the sly foxes, I could have been like them. I shook my head no, and then yes, and ran off.

I would have been content to think of that book, the getting of it, as something always in the future: the book, myself, John Blake, his big house, my name in scripted black ink, and whatever dangerous secrets were in the book itself, all made safe and flexible in the future tense.

But Nancy, hearing it all, told her mother and her mother told mine. Momma was only a girl herself, I know now, and just couldn't get it out of her mind.

"Cathryn, if you don't get yourself up to Mr. Blake's house, he'll forget he ever promised you that book."

"He won't forget," I had said. I knew. Playing "Little Sally Waters," I was in the middle. *Sitting in a saucer.* It was beginning to rain again. The moist faces, pink arms, *Rise, Sally, rise,* scraps of color, *wipe your weeping eyes,* chanting, *turn to the east, turn to the west,* as the circle of children stretched melody *turn to the very one* to whine, to demand *that you love the best,* I had seen him again. Between us the rags of children, behind him the cool sky. I thought I might burst through the ringing singers and throw my arms around John Blake. But I threw my arms around Nancy. And when I looked for him again I was a segment of that wavering wheel of song: I saw fragments of pale sky, part of the gray warehouse, our own little houses spinning past, as frail as the row of mailboxes thrust on posts above the board fences, the brown, wet weeds and puddles that kept creeping into our game, but he was gone. I should have chosen him. Then he would not have pursued me since that time—since I was a not-yet five-year-old child.

"He might forget," my mother had insisted as though it were a threat. "He's got lots of money. He's got his eye on things and knows which little children deserve something more in life." I wanted to hear how it was I deserved more, I wanted an account of my qualities, but Momma went on to list his. "God knows it just broke his heart to lose one son in the war and the other son, son's wife, and baby girl in a fatal car accident. Just lucky little Fletcher was with John. And now his own wife gone to, well, some say it was alcohol, but I say it was more to it than that. Plenty more." I didn't notice what she said for awhile; she didn't expect me to.

Then I heard Fletcher's name again. Fletcher was taller,

older, seldom in town, and knew my name. On Christmas Eve I had dropped a mitten and he'd said, "It's Cathryn's." And Effie Blake had run over and stuffed it in my pocket. John Blake's wife; Fletcher's grandmother. I saw her translucent skin, could almost see her bones through it as she poked the mitten into my pocket. And then before Christmas could come round again, she was dead.

I wasn't interested in the dead, but in the tall boy who had pronounced my name. "Where's Fletcher now?" I asked Momma.

"Away at school. He only comes home for the holidays." Thus, Fletcher became linked with rabbits and colored eggs, hot Julys, and cold, gifted Christmases. Feasts and ribbons. Excess and disappointment. Tension and color. And all the animals on the edges of time, in the slots of holidays—donkeys who could speak in the presence of the baby Jesus, artistic rabbits, strings of quails and snakes generated by heat, lambs wearing crowns and little blankets with mysterious marks. The occasions of seeing Fletcher and his attendants.

"That poor little soul," she said the way she must have heard it from Aunt Teresa, "no momma or daddy."

It sounded like he was an angel. And how easily I would have forfeited my mother just then for that illusion of grace. I was almost five and I wanted to decide when to wear my shoes. Now what would I forfeit to bring her back?

Finally my mother had said, "Cathryn, you can't put it off anymore. Go today and get that book Mr. Blake's got for you. You never know," she said to herself, "he might put a five-dollar bill inside it."

The getting of a book felt almost ominous. I knew that the faded white paint over the green bricks on Atkins street said Coca-Cola. I wished for a hieroglyph of style, some way each word could wear its own meaning out plain, like the scroll and fun of Coca-Cola, ultimately my seduction into literacy.

"Write my name like Coca-Cola," I'd asked my dad as he sat at the table.

"No, you keep to printing for now," my mother meddled.

He smiled, "Learn how these letters sound. Then I'll take you up to the drugstore and buy you a Coca-Cola."

So there was a code. Cat, Coca-Cola, and me. Pencil, pig, and paper. Penny. Dad, dog, dish. Momma, man, moon. Spoon—no. I began to crack apart words in my dad's crooked printing and the sounds threw up nonsense like wild movies, bits of dreams, suddenly projected on the modest stage of the kitchen table.

"What about that Coke now?" said my mother.

"I gotta get on to work," he said.

Momma didn't say anything. As soon as he shut the door behind him, she sat down and painted her nails. She washed me and changed my dress as though I were still a baby. She polished my shoes with the washcloth and attached a bit of crinkle-tie, saved from Christmas, into my hair. She put on lipstick, looked at herself awhile, then looked quickly into her purse and snapped it shut. We put on our good coats. I knew when to be quiet. And we went hand in hand to the drugstore.

She couldn't make up her mind about sitting down. I climbed right up onto the red cushion and held the varnished ridge of the counter while my mother stood close, as though I'd fall.

"Sit down," I said.

She climbed onto the next stool. "We'd like two Cokes, please." Her voice was so quiet, I reached for her hand. "Don't feel shy," she said to me, getting it backwards.

Peter Barclay gave us our Cokes. There, in frosty letters, on the side of my glass was my Rosetta Stone, *Coca-Cola*. We sucked on our straws, glancing toward the magazines on one side and the remedies on the other. Momma picked up her glass with her bright nails. I wished my gnawed and soggy straw was lipsticked like hers.

She tipped her head and smiled. "You know, it was like you found out what reading was. All of a sudden. You won't start kindergarten for another few weeks. I never saw anything like that." And she looked just like the beautiful girls in the pictures above the mirror, laughing over their shapely glasses of the elixir, Coca-Cola.

Peter saw it too. He leaned toward her, resting his white-shirted arms on the damp counter, and I turned invisible. I spent my time guessing at the words etched, embossed, on everything accessory to the substantiation of that moment, Coca-Cola. That must have been when Peter started coming to visit her. It just seemed natural, after he became the assistant pastor of the Baptist Church, that he'd keep coming.

"You better," Momma began again the next day, "go get that book John Blake's got for you."

"I'm going today," I said, as though it had been a plan.

"I'll walk you there."

"No, it's only up the hill behind Randy and Carl's house. I can go myself," I said importantly. I wanted to be sure I got that book. I didn't want him to give it instead to my mother, who had invested so much time thinking about it.

She insisted on folding my socks; she sprinkled my hair with the pop bottle she used on her ironing and wrapped damp curls around her fingers; she tied the bow on the back of my blue-checked dress five times, as if she thought I were a gift to the old man, not that he was going to give something to me.

"What if he forgot?" I asked her. "I'll just say hi."

"You just be real sweet. Who knows what he could slip in the pages of a book."

"He's kind of old."

"He's not so old. Maybe fifty."

"Fifty hundred."

When I got to John's backyard, Fletcher's old shepherd welcomed and announced me.

"Well, Catie. Catie did. Catie did come to see us."

When I heard "us" I thought of Fletcher and looked around, hoping he'd appear.

"Look at what Sally Cat has here," he said to me. "Fletcher's always leaving stray animals with me. And Sally Cat was a surprise package. Look what she's done."

John picked up the new kittens out of their box and put them in my lap, sliding his hand out from under each of them, leaving squirming bags of skin, their eyes shut in their new skulls, on my dress. Sally Cat, the momma, complained and switched her tail. He tried to divert her with a saucer of milk.

When I got home, Momma said, "Well, let's see it."

She looked all the way through it page by page, ignoring the book, looking for something alien in it. "Sure you didn't let anything drop out of it, honey?"

"No. It's stories. *From Other Lands*."

"Well, it's a nice book," she said, as though something were my fault. "Mr. Blake wrote your name here in the front. Did he ask you to come back?"

"He asked me to marry him," I said.

She laughed, tossing the book on the table. Then she looked at me through her lashes when she peeled the potatoes. "Did he touch you?" she whispered, transmuting her voice, the words, to fit inside the *snick snick* of the potato peeler.

"Only touch your ear with your elbow," I answered, showing I knew all the rules of touching, telling, testing.

"How'd you like his house?" she asked, dumping the potatoes into cold water.

"He's got papers all over the place. And little dolls made of glass. The lace on their dresses is glass."

"Those were his wife's china dolls," she explained as though she'd been there herself. I went outside, granting her no more vicarious glimpses into her misaligned desire and her hope for me beyond her own damaged fortune.

•

Oh, Momma, that early time forced itself onto the future. And whenever I come here in the woods I think of you and long ago.

It was the day before I started school for the first time, and the only time Momma and I went walking together in the woods, this little patch of sleep apart from our decrepit houses, from the big fading houses like John's, from the college, from the collapsing manufacturers of candy and cheese, all of them splayed and smothering the agricultural land that was their source. It was then that we saw these purple spires and she gave me her imperfect, incomplete little mystery of the foxes and their gloves.

"These are foxgloves. The foxes come and take these and wear them for gloves."

It was not much of a story. Oh, Momma, you never had enough in your head. Or maybe that's just an idea John put in my head.

That night Dad worked late and she lay down beside me to comfort me before the first day of school. Or to comfort herself. "Shall I read you one of the stories in your book? It's called 'Melissina's Message: Stories from the Far Wall.' "

She showed me the table of contents, which she said named the stories. I chose the one that began with C.

"It's 'Carolina, the Gypsy Girl,' " she said. And she read it to me.

> *Once there was a man about to leave for a journey and said to his wife, "Don't let the gypsies take the cow, our beautiful Carolina, or," he added, "yourself. Just offer them a trinket and they'll be on their way."*
>
> *He had been gone three days and three nights. Carolina and her mother brought in the wash from the lines and, at the top of the hill, the woman saw a gypsy wagon appear, and tied behind it, her own sweet brown cow.*
>
> *"Hide in the basket," she said to Carolina, wrapping her in the tablecloth, flinging wash on top, "and be very still."*

The gypsy wagon stopped before the house and a man, dark and rosy and quick, was at her door.

"Our cow," she bravely countered his smile and his knife.

"Would you like to buy the cow?" he laughed and almost touched her hair.

"Yes," she said, remembering her husband's word that they'd leave for a trinket.

"Where's your coin?" he teased her, and cut off a button from her bodice.

"I have no money. We can trade," she said. She offered him her dear little milk jug, the picture of her grandmother, the gloves she wore at her wedding.

"I will choose," suggested the gypsy. "Whatever I choose is mine, and I give you the cow in trade."

"Yes," said the woman; she felt his breath as he bent close, examining her own gold locket. She showed him the pink china bowl, the silver spoon, and let her skirt drape over the laundry basket.

"You are so generous," he winked and stroked her skirt with the blade of his knife. "My people need simple things. We need clothes. I'll take the laundry basket."

He picked up the basket and laughed. "Come, untie your cow."

"Wait. I have other clothes. I have a velvet dress. I'll give you that."

"No. I take only what's in the basket."

She followed him to the cart.

"I know how to find a house's treasure," he said to her softly. He pulled Carolina from the tangle of clothing. She reached for her mother and then clung to the gypsy who held her tight.

"Take the cow," he commanded.

"Keep the cow," the woman cried. "Carolina will have the milk."

"Good-bye then," grinned the man.

"Only let me have a lock of her hair," she begged.

The gypsy, with his knife, cut a curl from Carolina's head. It coiled like a snake in the mother's palm.

"What do you trade?" the gypsy demanded, for a lock of my child's hair?"

She gave him the milk jug, the picture of her grandmother, and the gloves from her wedding day.

And the gypsy started to drive away, but Carolina's mother called after him, "Take me too."

"So," he said as he pulled her to his side, "you choose the gypsy life. What do you trade for the chance to come on my cart?"

She had brought him the velvet dress, the silver spoon, the pink bowl, but he told her to keep the gold locket at her neck.

They rode for a day and a half, slow enough for the cow. Then they met the other gypsies at a low, green camp.

The others heard the story of how he traded for Carolina and laughed, their teeth gleaming in the fire.

The oldest gypsy woman said, "Carolina is wise enough to be silent, I will teach her to read the stars, the cards, the eyes of strangers. The woman is not clever enough for the gypsy life."

The woman wept and gave Carolina her gold locket. "This is all I have. Remember me," she said.

And they gave her some bread, a little cup, a length of cloth, and sent her back to her house to wait for her husband.

Carolina always remembered her mother and learned many other things only the gypsies know.

I fell asleep, rolling smug and snug with the gypsies, even though it was my own tearful mother who was with me in my bed. I wonder how it would have changed for us if John had not sent that book, that story, to corrupt our connection? Did the past give order to what became and what will be? Maybe it was inevitable; I went off to school the next day.

Here by the foxgloves, though, I don't think it was inevitable.

I hear Fletcher. On his way to find me.

"Cathryn. Ca tha ryn!"

I don't care to answer him.

Behind this clutch of foxglove and fern, shadowed in a stand of fir, I discover a deer skull.

"Ca Tha Ryn. I know you can hear me."

I see through the deer's eyeless cranium into the brain cavity—a gorgeous wasp- and ant-polished chamber—which has captured stars of thistledown. Wisps of whispers. Like the ideas we get after we're gone. Death's dreams.

"Come on now," Fletcher's still bellowing. "Cathryn, honey."

Those downed achenes will never sprout in the absented mind of the animal. They are there like stilled dancers in a silent, marble ballroom. Or, more like stilled thinkers in a celestial classroom. Maybe stilled lovers in a vast, metaphysical bedroom.

Fletcher's coming over the ridge. I sit down by the foxglove, sticking my fingers up into the hanging trumpets as I always believed, from the time my mother told me, the foxes stuck their paws. I once waited a long time for the foxes to come to their emporium and try on their gloves. I wanted to see where they went after that. What occasioned their fox-gloved rituals. Foxes, after all, so well-dressed without them; what ceremony demanded purple-ruffled, black-spotted, silken mittens?

"Cathryn!" Fletcher's coming hard over the last hill and not even winded. "It's time."

I have three fingers suited up in fox-glove blossoms, when I notice the factor of time on the stalks. The bells ascend the shafts in a sequenced pattern of ripeness. The lowest corollas are already withered, the uppermost are yet green-globed futures. Past, present, future. The foxglove spires cluster their notations on time. Counting on their fingers. Digitalis. Hurrying the hearts contemplating death. That must be...

"There you are. Come on now, sweetheart."

...must be why they are able to regulate the unruly, and maybe why they wither so quickly when they're picked.

"Cathryn, don't do this now. You know if there was anyone else to take care of Grandfather, I'd have spared you this." Fletcher changes his awkward shadow to warm flesh around me.

"Fletcher," I ask into his close face, "do you think maybe when the foxes wear these, the others tell them it's a mistake, and the foxes answer, 'Aw, it's just a way to pass the time'?"

"Let's go now, Cathryn." He kisses a glow into my cool-as-blue neck and pulls me up.

"It was a joke," I explain, following him back over the deer walk. "Fox pass. Fox paws." He says nothing. "Ignorant manners. Like when Aunt Teresa used to wear those white gloves all through luncheon at Miss Wilson's."

Fletcher asked, "You got your things packed?"

"No gloves."

He says nothing. I punch him on his broad back. Fletcher's so handsome, even following his anger in the sun, I like him. "Shit, Fletcher, you never get a joke."

He turns around. "You know, Cathryn, if he weren't so sick, you could go back to graduate school. And you will, as soon as..."

He can't force the words of it all into that little flat silence he holds by his teeth, so I fill up my silence with crying. "How can you expect me to go? Now? How can I believe I'll ever get back to school if I leave it now? How can you expect me to be in the same house with John? Only six months ago he was trying to bully me or bribe me into our marrying immediately, you changing your work, me stopping my study." I don't tell Fletcher, to oversee the breeding of his succession.

"Six months is enough to change the world if six days was enough to make it."

I remember when I thought Fletcher's common words must be threads unraveled from uncommon depths. Just to give myself permission for the pleasures of his hard-baked flesh, his soft manners, the animals he keeps crouched in the bare tremble of his touch.

"I think he's dying," Fletcher says. "So you just wait. You just take care of him. Keep his suffering down, clean up. You can boil water, perennial college girl. You can make his meals."

"Hire someone."

"You know he's fired anyone who can manage it. It's his way of saying he needs someone more than a stranger."

"Fletcher, if you don't care about my learning, you don't care about my soul."

He changes his mood as we walk from rolling earth back into shadowed trees. I love your soul. From the beginning. I think Grandfather always saw it, too."

"Doctor Davis says the desire to exalt the woman is ultimately the enslavement of her."

"Who do you think paid for your classes with Davis?"

"Oh, he only set up that big scholarship so that Miss Wilson's estate wouldn't grant me my freedom. 'For Local Student with Family Hardship and Demonstrating Academic Promise.' He just wants to own me."

Fletcher laughs. "Remind me to never offer a scholarship. You're right. He wants to own everything he thinks is wonderful. He always says you're just like him. But I don't want to own you," he says, stopping and holding me, "I'll call Mark Edie and tell him to replace me on the research team. I'll take care of Grandfather. I won't do this to you."

And I'm tricked by my desire to nurture Fletcher, my orphan who has raised up our mysterious love, so I finally insist, "I'll nurse John; but it will be a bitter broth I serve."

"Just let me get my research assistants established, then I'll come back and take over. You know, Cathryn, the results of this study are going to be crucial for establishing environmental policy; Cathryn, you're doing this for the trillium, the hawk, the..."

"The fox." I've never heard him resort to such rhetoric before; but even the way he's fooling himself more than me, makes me love the profile of his nose more; makes me love his concentration on his work in spite of his grandfather's scorn and interference.

How can I solve the contradiction? Dr. Davis says women always end up capitulating to the patriarchy, strengthening it out of their impulses to reform it. How can I love Fletcher without giving in to the tyranny of John? "He's a mean old man," I complain.

"He's not so much mean as just old now."

"I'm not going to sit there and wait for him to die." And all I've done for Fletcher. I took Botany just to please him, and Biology all the way through the mammals, and now he's willing to send me off to John. I see, Fletcher, that he is your grandfather. But he is also father to the child I would not have. Is he not closer kin to me?

"Maybe we can help him recover. Maybe he'll get back his health," Fletcher says lamely.

Fletcher will never know.

He stops to scan the town from our hilltop. We look toward Parks Hall on one plump hill; John's house obscured on the other. "Fletcher, what do you think Time is?" I stop the silence, just before the last cluster of trees stop.

"I think we have time," he deliberately teases me, pulling me down and pressing me between the earth and himself. And I think Fletcher has the answer: to hear it wrong, in order to have the freedom to make it up, is the only escape from commonplace time.

Fletcher strokes away my gooseflesh, shields me from the wind, until I reach his temperature and I think for a moment a fox is near; we cast our flesh into the patterns of the images in our minds, disremembering our alienation for that brief eternity.

When I open my eyes, the sky has gathered closer, drawn toward our scent.

If Fletcher knew how John had hurt me, would it damage him? I haven't been in John's house since that day, and he thinks it's because we're quarreling over John's interference in our lives. That, too. He's going to die and we'll never have to meet him again at the Casa Mariposa for the taste of avocado or shrimp or cinnamon on our tongues, never again the taste of coercion or tension from John's presence. His imminent future already has cast his shadow back, black, into the past.

If only Fletcher had been there when I had gone to the house to thank John for my first year on the scholarship, to brag about my essays, and to quote my professors. I hadn't realized how bitter he was toward the university. School and Fletcher—a sudden and lovely man—had sheltered me from too much grief over Mother, or much awareness of anyone else.

I had made tiny strawberry tarts and brought them to John that day. He placed them on a small china plate.

We stood awkwardly in his dining room, light barely falling on the cabinets of china and glass, shrouded by dust and drapes, this and the library forbidden to his cleaning woman. I stepped behind one of the horsehair upholstered chairs, beyond the table, a massive oval of burled walnut.

"What a beautiful plate," I said.

"One of Effie's collection," he said. Does he still grieve? I wondered. "The rare ones. She hunted them out." He suddenly spilled the tarts off the dessert dish. "Do you want to look at it?" he asked in parody of the solicitous host, offering the plate instead of the food. I looked at the cracked shells of the little pies.

John had picked up the plate by the span of his hand. "She loved these little things; that's all that would bring her out of it sometimes," he said with his fingertips at the rim of the plate clocking the departure of her mind, the return of her memory.

The light changed on the plate as he brought it closer. Latticework and vines, trumpeting blossoms, an oddly painted tower. Then, as he held it higher, catching the light, the plate glinted a halo and John's face darkened. Effie was forgotten again; I failed to wonder, at that time, whatever it was in the painted porcelain, the Dresden dolls, that might have given her brief pause in her unnamed torment.

Instead, I was flooded with the acrid recall of my first semester on the hill, World Civilization, with Dr. Michelson, who liked to give us to the easy shocks of education and who began each class with a reading from "the ancient voices." And, we learned, as he tried to unnerve us, that in the Middle Kingdom, Set demanded intercourse with Horus. Horus told his mother, Isis, who advised her son to position himself so that Set would "enjoy it exceedingly" and Horus might secretly receive the semen of Set between his fingers and throw it into the stream. Then Isis instructed Horus to provide some of his own semen, which she cunningly fed to Set on a lettuce leaf. Before the court of Thoth, that great god of learning, Set declared his dominance; but his semen testified from the bottom of the marsh, and Horus's semen rose up in Set and issued from his forehead as a golden disc. Thoth rejoiced and seized the disc as his own ornament. The moon. "And there's a mother for you," Dr. Michelson had joked, drawing attention from the other players.

As John Blake held Effie's little possession like a trophy of his own strength, he transmuted her china into the incongruity, the contradiction, of ancient Egypt's phallic disc. Why was I frightened? How long had we stood poised?

John saw my fright.

He brought the gilt-edged dish down and crushed it beneath his hand, scratching the table. Effie's plate smashed, and John grasped a sickle-shaped shard and thrust it toward my throat. He squeezed the crescent of bone china and drew his own blood, which trickled onto his shirt cuff. I watched the stain spread and was silent and refused to move. I remembered his wife again in her broken plate. I had never had time to think about her before; but in this long moment I might have searched her out.

"Run," something hissed in the house.

"I wouldn't hurt you," he said finally. "I would never hurt you." He dropped his new-moon weapon and caressed my face with his bleeding hand. "I would never hurt you,

Catie," he wept. When I ran, he threw me onto the carpet, a dark oriental so finely figured it kept the secret. He tore my clothes, and broke my tooth, and raped me. Quickly.

And just as quickly returned to his standard manners, ushering me through the kitchen, "Here, Catie, why don't you wear this coat home? You'll be more comfortable. And take these strawberries to your mother. Tell her they're the first from my garden. And," he looked at me unrepentant, "this will not recur. You are not to fear me. This was for one moment. You may forget it," he said as though he were granting me a favor.

Had he forgotten my mother was dead, or was he trying to manipulate my fear, my self-doubt, or to raise up my guilt over my mother, larger than his was over me? The strawberries in my broken tarts had been from my own garden. It wouldn't occur to John I could keep my own strawberry bed.

I was able to walk home; it was not discovered; doesn't that mean it didn't happen? He almost granted me the favor of amnesia.

If, though, I were able to erase that horror, then I would forget, as well, moments with Fletcher. Flawed as he and I are, our limited good must be celebrated and recalled, like a minor note in the liturgy.

We return just before he must board his plane for Washington. And I take myself up to John's.

"Shouldn't my grandson have stayed around to mop the green bile of my dying?"

"Fletcher took a temporary position with the government," I explain again. "Partly as a kindness to Doctor Edie. You know it's an honor to be part of the research team. He can't get out of it now." I amend, "You won't die."

"I'm still too much alive to want to hear wild stories that I'm one of the immortals. What's he doing now? Chasing tales of prairie dogs? Or tallying up goose eggs? Gee-ology or Forced-tree? Maybe you better watch out, Catie, maybe he's really studying Wild Life."

I don't respond to the taunts John's been using on Fletcher since high school. John has never been funny; why with his last breath does he keep trying?

He suddenly starts talking again, "You expect me to say, 'Cate, forgive me.' I won't do it. Stop whining around about your precious university and really learn something. You are here to midwife to death. Of course, death has already arrived. You'll have to wet-nurse it until it's strong enough to pack me off."

The old fool has no wisdom to call upon in his last hours; he will resort to childish blasphemies, imprecise obscenities. And he will not give up mocking me for my pleasure in the education he used to subsidize. John's house on one hillock, the college on another; but the college spread, "festered," John said. And by the time old Mrs. Tenny and Miss Wilson had bequeathed their property behind John's to the college, it was a university and John was almost surrounded. His own considerable library was never supplemented by borrowing from the academic one, and his will specifies, he told us once during one of his dinner harangues, that his books go to a public library five states away.

His breathing catches up with his next attack on me. Finally he says, "What if time itself moves toward entropy, not just the sagging of earth, but time itself? What if it runs down before I do? We'll be stuck here, won't we, Cate?"

I'm not going to answer.

"We're just marking time," he says, trying to pull me with his weakening grasp into his abyss, "before the ultimate passage—death—the only proof of time's play."

He sees he'll have to make more ruthless his strategies for conversation, as I will not succumb to entertaining him: "Do you miss your mother?"

I say nothing.

"I do," he says. Is he chuckling or choking? Let him go.

After Dad left, Momma must have scanned her stars and saw no seasons coming, no shifts of light, no falling stars or wishes. She took the pills. And who was sorry to see a spent girl of thirty-seven, sweetness thickened into a stale pudding, succumb to her silent embarrassment? She chose that winter, the heat off but all the lights on. She couldn't feel anymore, but she could see. Was that her message to us all? More so than her note to me: *Dear Cathryn, When I'm gone there will be enough money, I figure, to put you through college. I think that money tree we planted is just about to bloom.* She was a dim jokester, like an insufficiently prepared after-dinner speaker. *I'm sorry I won't be there to see all the things you do. I really do love you. And, you know, I feel really honored to have been part of the chain that brought you here, and pray to God you'll keep it going. Please forgive me. Love, Mother.*

Peter Barclay stood at the graveside, his voice buckled with grief, and the wind flung the bits of his eulogy against the traffic down the hill. A semi hauled away the Amen and the mourners didn't know when to stop staring at the slush seeping into their church shoes.

I miss her as acutely now as when I swallowed all the pennyroyal capsules with bitter tea and willed it to work. I imagined my mother finding me folded over and putting me into bed. I might have been pregnant; it might have been Fletcher's child; it might have been John's. Worrying so much about the father, I did not think I was the mother. And I hallucinated the ghost of *my* mother, who had left me. I vomited, cramped, and bled. There was no child; I purged myself of the imp in my mind stamped in the image of John Blake.

Now John dimly watches me and realizes I exorcised him long ago.

But he keeps on, "Catie, bug, bring me that little morocco book five shelves up on the north wall."

In the library, on the north wall, five shelves up, a dozen copies of *Melissina's Message.* I stopped to consider the book that had snared me so many years ago. Were these multiple copies for other little girls? Was I part of a collection? Then I noticed the odd publisher, Tower House. And I finally recognized the author, Job Lakehn. So, all this time he wanted to be found out by those academics on the other hill. They didn't, or didn't care to, find him out. The unsung, undiscovered author. His vanity publications never admired by those squatting and sprawling on the opposite hill.

"Here it is, John." I take him the book which sharpens his dwindling wakefulness.

"Read to me. The third one in. It's for you."

I should have known which one he'd choose. But I give him that much pleasure, the miniscule power of his words emerging from my throat. Could he know that I can hear Momma reading it to me? I will not permit him to think that his story affects me; but that means I must suppress the echo of Mother's voice. Has John won again?

Carolina always remembered her mother and learned many other things only the gypsies know.

I finish the story and close the book.

"Well, Cate, what do you think?"

I change his pillowcase. He grazes my breast.

So this, at last, is the deathbed wish. The old cliché of the insecure writer—he wants to hear that he is one. "I wouldn't be able to judge it," I demur.

"Well look at it 'til you can. You put off marrying my grandson, denying me the chance to get a look at the offspring so I can see if any will resemble me, just so you can go on collecting degrees," he says contemptuously, producing more yellow spittle I'm forced to wipe away. "You hurt Fletcher beyond repair—and just to spite me."

I throw the tissue in the basket and leave the room.

"Take your nap, John. You'll feel better this afternoon. You can dictate a new story, I'll write it down."

"No more tales," he says as though he wants me to be sorry.

I leave the house, shutting the door carefully so John can't hear. I go to the only place where I can be alone. The foxes have not come yet.

I will not hear John's liquid breath near the trees, three hills remote from the house, from his insistent, feeble touches, and from my own weariness with washing away death's stains. But his cruel story inserts itself. It's as though he wrote it years ago just so he'd have it when I wanted to escape being his nurse. A woman's breasts must seem a property claim to a man like John, of all her sweet obligations, and all her milky promises to him. And, to a man like Fletcher, what do they pledge?

I remember Fletcher was eighteen; I was still a girl, fourteen. He seemed so exotic. He had everything: serious eyes, broad shoulders, dead parents, a whole range of bird-calls and animal cries which he said really worked. I had loved him every glance I got of him when he came to his grandfather's between one boarding school after another. I thought he was stuffed with secrets, esoteric rumblings that no one who'd been stuck at home, going to public school, hounded by breathing, meddlesome parents, could hope to know. He only told me one secret though. Enough. Intimate enough. Grotesque enough to seal our love.

"At the last school," he had confided to me, "they made us pray more than they made us study. One day they gave us each a bun and told us it was St. Agnes's breast."

"What?" I had hissed, shocked to hear that word from Fletcher, and so close to the words *pray* and *study*.

"St. Agnes," he told me, "was so beautiful and so good they pulled off her breasts to torture her."

"Who?"

"Pagans."

We were silent awhile. "Then they killed her," he continued. "So we each had a breast—I mean a bun—with a
raisin on top," he even blushed at that. "We were supposed
to eat it and remember and pray."

"What did you do?"

"I took it back to my room and put it under the bed.
It dried out and I broke it up for the birds."

"How big was it?"

"Life-size."

And we both blushed. I wondered if my own compared
to the saint's. So did Fletcher. We walked for a while, and
then he kissed me shyly, brushing my own yeasty offering.
It was another three years before he kissed me again.

And then two more years when he found me walking,
thinking about Momma. What had brought him home out
of sequence, during regular days without holy, or healing
power? He came into the ordinary time and so came
genuinely into my life. And he took me over the road his
own momma had been killed on—did he think of her?—or
his father?—his baby sister?—and on into Riddleyville
where we made love for two days. We drove back and no
one had missed us. No wonder they've always compared
love and death; the same road, the philosopher said, goes
both up and down. And now it's been ten years. How many
breasts baked, consecrated, hidden, broken, offered up. This
is my flesh. Don't ask for more. Don't scatter me to the
winds and call to the greedy birds.

Don't offer me up to your grandfather.

I return to John and look in his oddly and coolly bright
room.

The old man's mouth sags open; the sandman, death's
helpful second cousin, has tried to seal the rims of his eyes
shut. Beyond is the goblet I'd brought him at mid-morning.
Holding it, to please him with the clatters of crystal, ice,
and sparklng water, he'd said, "Last rites?"

"It's beautiful."

"Last rites. From a damned girl. And a damned one at that."

Am I damned? In his universe. His soon to be extinguished. And will there still be a bleak—sunk like the past—universe of his making, in which some image of me will be captured, pale, servile, and damned?

Ice remains in the glass, measured proof that I haven't been gone too long, or proof that death's touch rules.

Light has sprung through ice, water, glass—all metamorphoses of itself—into a burst of broken rainbow vibrating spines of shattered nerve. The spiny prism looks like a gift in death's room. Perhaps it's the angel of death; I could catch her like a moth, to buzz in my hand.

"Where've you been?" asks the noisy corpse.

"Outside."

"Did you see Death come up the walk? It seems to have escaped from me."

"Only myself."

"I should have guessed. Death will come to me as a silky, sullen girl."

I am not a caricature in his life; he will not violate me in this way—by forcing me into his pageant.

"The temple of death," he said, trying to touch my face and missing. "Behind your eyes the temple."

Tonight I sit by him as he rasps and wheezes. He is drowning and drying, all at once; death is so difficult for him. At one point he comes out of the delirium and can see me, desiring me as life itself. And I go down to him, and press myself close beside him, our sudoric mists, his icy and mine fevered, mingle like a cloud around us. And I think, in the soft, ruffled bed I had made for him, of the blossom bedroom Zeus devised for Hera when she diverted him from the Acheans in the battle below. And I feel John's final attempt to grasp onto the living, and I warm him all night, like Jesus pressed to the leper. Those old quarreling and depleted gods, from all around the ancient crescent, incongruously converge, enlivened by a mortal's death. I place my hand, like a child once more, in his, now a cup made of his death-tensed muscle spasms. And I see, as the close bell of night opens into mauve, the black spots he must be seeing as he keeps opening his wandering eyes; so I put my mouth close to his, letting him borrow slight ribbons of my breath; and I can feel the faint electric charge of those black spots in the cup of his hand cramped around my numb fingers.

I accompany him as far as I can into that new place. Then I waken back into my own life, wash him for the last time, bathe and change, and call Fletcher, "Fletcher, please come now."

"It's done," he says.

"Yes."

And I wait, wondering if we can rescue for ourselves a time that will cure the old entropic one. Fletcher, remember when you used to come to me for the holidays? The holiday once was the rescue of entropy.

Hope Chest

Dolores was waiting to get married. She had been waiting since she was fourteen; blood had come and made her eyes and stomach twitch in surprise and fear, but her mother had said, "Soon you'll be married and then things will be different." Dolores had gone down into that waiting like a fork into gray dishwater. She rested on the bottom of a blank expectancy; and her mother, Mrs. Rasmussen, and her brother, Irving, who sharpened saws in the shed, waited for Dolores to change their lives.

Dolores was heading toward her three-hundredth menstruation and could fold and pin the rags expertly and was proud of the way she soaked them dark red and made them beautiful until they dried and stiffened. Her mother had taught her to wrap them carefully in newspaper, almost like little gifts, and put them in the burning barrel. Dolores lit matches to them and the fire took the newspapers first and fast, savoring the cloths that held some other metamorphosis of their own nature. Dolores always watched the fires until they were completely out. "Then we know you won't burn up the whole valley," her mother had often repeated. When Dolores watched the fire she tried to understand more about the secret she had found out: blood is like fire. "Blood is like fire," she had said to Mrs. Rasmussen, who responded, "Dolores, don't let no one hear you talkin' like that. You're doin' real good." Dolores thought if she did what she should and didn't say the things her mother was able to divine as mistakes, then the marriage would spring up like a surprise.

Dolores was having a birthday. She had learned from Mrs. Rasmussen that birthdays were a sign that the waiting was running out. They didn't bother to count them up any more than they would have counted up the seasons of the blackberries. When they blossomed, it was spring, when they ripened, it was fall. Dolores had her birthday in the spring, Mrs. Rasmussen in the fall. Irving's was in the dead of winter. Nothing was pinned on Irving.

Dolores sat on the wooden chair and watched her mother bake her birthday cake. She wound a damp strand of hair around her fingers until her mother told her, "Stop playing with your hair, Dolores. You're lucky to have that pretty yellow hair, and lucky to have a momma to brush it for you every day. I'm using my tomato soup recipe. Tomato soup is the surprise ingredient. No one can ever guess. I got the recipe from Mrs. Brooks. I copied it out and pasted it in your recipe book in your hope chest." She spoke to Dolores as though she didn't already know these things. "Okay, Dolores, you go run down the road and ask Ethel and Willie to come and have some cake with us after supper."

"They might be busy."

"Go on now, Dolores, you do as I say."

Dolores took the paths through the blackberries higher than their house, around the gully, and came up through the backyard of Ethel and Willie. They had a chicken house and hens always laying; they had fruit trees that never had a bad year; they even had a little birdbath and the birds liked it. "It's a good thing, Ethel likes everything clean,"

Dolores said aloud, thinking she would have a place like this when she got married.

She stood and looked through the screen door until Ethel saw her and acted pleased to have company. Ethel brought her in saying, "We were just about to have a little toast and coffee. Sure glad you came by."

The kitchen smelled of bleach. Dolores looked in the sink and saw dishrags swirling so slowly, most wouldn't have noticed that they were moving at all. "They look like they're dying."

Ethel said, "Oh, Dolores, I've just been bleachin' out my dishrags. Does it bother you, honey? Here, I'll just let it out," and Ethel wrung out the dishrags and spread them out on her stainless towel rack as the chlorine water complained and disappeared down the drain. She wiped her hands on her big apron, and then pulled Dolores and a chair together.

Willie came in and said, "Well, Dolores, glad you came. Now that means we'll get to have apple butter with our toast."

Dolores knew it was a joke and she laughed. She watched Ethel work like a matter-of-fact magician, spreading a clean cloth on the chrome table, putting out china cups and saucers, glass luncheon plates, a bouquet of daffodils in the center, napkins folded into triangles, silver knives and spoons, butter, two kinds of jelly, cheese, and apple butter, all in painted dishes and little hand-labeled jars. Ethel brought a tray of toast from the oven and buttered them all before Dolores could have done one. She stacked them up in two rows and sliced them through so they were triangles like the napkins.

"You used to work in a restaurant," said Dolores.

"Yep," said Willie, "that's what I married her for. Good hot food and in a hurry."

Dolores missed this joke, but laughed with them. She knew she couldn't get a job in a restaurant. She knew she'd have to think about this when she was by herself; so she dropped it in the big bin in her mind that held the paraphernalia of her reveries.

Dolores watched Ethel pour the coffee. Her cup was white with violets painted on it; Willie's was green with lily of the valley; Ethel's was yellow with gold designs. It looked like daffodils.

"You should pour coffee in the daffodils," said Dolores.

"That wouldn't be very good, now would it?" said Ethel. Dolores was unhappy that Ethel didn't see her joke.

Willie, after a long pause, said, "They do look like cups and saucers, don't they, Dolores? I remember once hearing the fairies use 'em to drink from." Ethel and Willie glanced at each other. Dolores was sorry she had come. It was as though people were way up in trees dropping little plums of conversation to her, and she had to run after them and mostly miss.

"I don't believe in fairies," she said, trying to retrieve her dignity and her place at the table.

"Of course not," said Ethel. "We believe in God and His Only Begotten Son, Jesus Christ. Right, sweetheart?"

Willie winked at Dolores. She tried to drop this in, too, into that place for reconstructions and reconsiderations. But Dolores knew to answer yes to questions of that sort.

She tried to bite her toast so as not to reveal the shape of the inside of her mouth. Ethel and Willie seemed unconcerned, making gaping, fluted holes however they pleased. They were on to their third piece while Dolores still worked cautiously on her first.

"Have another, Dolores; have one with cheese. It's good for you."

Dolores dutifully put two little squares of cheese on a triangle, then coated it all with Ethel's dark, luminous blackberry jelly. She looked up at Ethel and saw she had made another error. She wanted to be home. She held the toast in both hands and didn't move.

"Go ahead, honey. You eat any way you like, and if you don't like somethin' you just leave it be."

Then Dolores couldn't figure out if she liked it or didn't, so she sat with the toast in her hands until Willie said, "Dolores likes your jelly as much as I do; I recall she helped me pick these berries." He consulted the label, confirming the vintage. Dolores bit into her cheese and jelly toast and liked it.

By the time Dolores finished, Willie was leaning back on his chair, Ethel resting her red elbows on the white tablecloth, sipping their coffee and discussing when they should stake the peas. Dolores kissed her napkin and said, "I have to go home."

"Well, thanks for comin' over, Dolores. That sure was nice of you." Everyone stood up and scooted chairs. Dolores got to the screen door and remembered.

"After supper is my birthday cake. My mother wants you to come. I want you to come." She quickly looked away and her face burned as they chirped in quick succession:

"Is your birthday today?"

"Happy birthday, honey."

"Well, Dolores, that's really nice of you. How old are you today?"

"Willie! Shame on you. Don't ever ask a lady her age. Right, Dolores? Dolores don't need to worry none anyway. I swear, she never ages; still looks like a girl. Well, we'll sure try to make it over, sweetheart, but I think my sister's comin' over from Auburn this evenin'. Wants me to help fit a dress to her. They just don't make patterns the same shape as my sister."

Dolores wondered why tears were trying to blind her; she didn't feel unhappy. She thought it would be lots easier if they didn't come.

Willie said, "Oh, I think we can come, Dolores. If those two old hens can't stop gossipin', do you think it'd be all right if I slip over for a little cake? I just can't pass up birthday cake. Besides, I heard once, if you get a piece of a pretty girl's birthday cake you have good luck for a whole year. I sure could use that luck."

"Okay," said Dolores with a bubble in her mouth, and left. She stopped around the corner of the house to wipe her eyes on her sweater. She didn't mean to hear them, but in early summer it's as easy to hear people through houses as in the same room with them.

"Oh Lord, Willie, you know I don't have a mean bone in my body, but I can't eat in that Rasmussen house. I've tried. Food sticks in my throat. It smells like the Goodwill in there."

"Well, Ethel, when someone asks you to be their birthday party, if you don't go, there ain't no party. I'm a goin' whether you come along or not. Will you fix her up a pretty birthday present?"

Ethel sighed, "That's easy. I'll just wrap her up somethin' for one of her hope chests."

"Now, Ethel, I don't want to. . ."

And Dolores fled past the plastic birdbath, the gray birds flickering in the water. Dolores knew that feathers resisted water, but she guessed the birds didn't know. She wondered if they wanted to be like people, or just who it was who taught them they should bathe.

"Well, you sure were a long time," said Mrs. Rasmussen. "Wait'll you see how pretty my cake is I made for you. I think I won't show you 'til the folks come."

"Ethel's got her sister comin' tonight; they're making a dress. So only Willie will be here."

"Oh, that's too bad. Ethel sure would 'preciate my cake. We'll send a big hunk of it back with Willie."

Dolores went back to her room and shut the door. She cried on her bed and held her hand against the safety pin and the soft folded cloth. It was warm, and a spot was forming through to the outer layer. When she stopped crying and felt relaxed, she took one of the newspapers from under the bed, folded another cloth, and changed it. She sat on the floor, liking to see her own blood. Only grown-up women did this, but not old ones like her mother. Only marriageable ones. It made her proof that she was not a child. "You still look like a girl," she heard Ethel's echo say. She knew that meant Ethel thought her on past girlhood, and she, without her "monthlies," would never know she had a way beyond it. Dolores wrapped the newspaper. Again, it looked like a gift and she was reminded that it was her birthday. This time she tried to recall how old she was. No one ever said anymore. She went into the kitchen and took a couple of wooden matches from the blue tin holder on the wall. Her mother looked at her, nodded, and said, "You're gettin' to be a woman. Pretty soon you'll be married. Then things'll change for us."

Dolores went to the burning barrel and lit the package. The paper burned quickly to a crisp negative of itself and went out. Dolores went back into the house, knowing that the cloth was not burned. She'd have to come back and make a hotter, hungrier fire.

She went back to her room and looked at her three hope chests.

The first was filled with linens. Mrs. Rasmussen had decorated them, one after the other, until no more could fit.

The second chest was a painted box Dolores had retrieved from the garage. It contained things she had scavenged, things she knew would be needed when she was married. It made her feel like she had made something out of nothing when she looked in it. It was crammed with spatulas, a pan, an eggbeater, even one of the salt and peppers from Mrs. Rasmussen's collection. There were six jelly glasses with enameled floral designs, three with clocks. Dolores had been urging Irving to finish off the last bit of jelly in the fourth. There were several beautiful plates without chips. Most she'd found in the garbage when people moved away. It made her feel resourceful to look in her box filled with her domestic potential.

The third chest was an old camelback trunk, filled

with baby clothes, all handmade by Mrs. Rasmussen—
nighties, blankets, and twenty-two embroidered bibs. Dolores liked the bibs best of all. On days like this, when there
seemed to be an ant colony under her skin, she'd take them
out, arrange them, and stack them up.

She took out the bibs now, though she was a little afraid
of the guillotine-like lid that sometimes came down with a
crisp sound, teasing Dolores for her hand or neck. She carefully closed the trunk so that the lid wouldn't hang over her.

On top was the bib with the fat yellow duck wearing
a ribboned bonnet and carrying a basket of purple variegated
daisies. That made Dolores feel better. She put them all in
her lap, shut her eyes, and tugged at one of the ties. She
opened her eyes and saw it was the bird with an umbrella
tucked under its wing, standing by two daffodils taller than
the bird. She could remember picking it out from the package of transfers, watching her mother iron over it and pull
the hot paper from the inked outline left on the cloth. She
had asked to iron it on, but her mother had said, "You'd
just smudge it. Don't stand so close when I've got a hot
iron." Suddenly the picture evoked a queasiness from which
Dolores wanted to escape; she wondered how that picture
had changed from the way it used to make her feel.

She drew out one more bib from her lap. It was the
one with the little Dutch boy and girl on each side of a
windmill. One arm of the windmill looked about to chop
through the cap of the Dutch girl. This picture had changed
too. She had never seen before the ominous overhanging
blade of the windmill. Dolores opened the trunk lid and
dumped the bibs in, drawing back from the trunk as it
crunched shut.

She sat without moving until Mrs. Rasmussen opened
the door of her room, stuck in her balding, bony head, and
said, "You want to pretty up before supper, Dolores? Hurry
up."

"When you poked your head around my door your hair
looked like cobwebs on an old skull," said Dolores.

"Don't act mean, just 'cause it's your birthday, girl. Get cleaned up."

Dolores dabbed at herself with a washcloth. Her mother had warned her against the bathtub during her time. She put on her dress with the violets, brushed her hair herself, and put in her favorite barrettes with the cats.

Mrs. Rasmussen came in the bathroom, took out the cats, rearranged Dolores's hair, and put in the barrettes with the doves.

"You'll like your birthday supper. I made you them seashell macaroni and sliced up a tomato and opened a jar of green beans. All what my little girl likes best."

Dolores wondered if those were what she liked best. Up close like this her mother didn't look like a skull. Dolores wanted to stay close to her.

No one spoke at the dinner table. They never did. Mrs. Rasmussen cleared away the dishes, wiped off the oilcloth. The three of them sat there and waited for Willie, and maybe for Willie and Ethel.

"I got you a present," said Irving.

"Let's see," said Dolores.

"Don't get ants in your pants," the old woman said.

"We gonna get cake?" asked Irving.

"Hold your horses," said their mother.

"Try to guess what I got you," Irving teased.

"Is it red?"

"You two, just sit still 'til company comes. You wear me out."

Irving looked at Dolores and touched a red square on his plaid shirt and shook his head no and grinned.

Dolores understood. She touched the green on the oilcloth table cover. Irving indicated no. She touched a violet on her dress.

"Don't touch yourself there, Dolores. Irving, hold still."

Irving picked up his cards and played solitaire. Mrs. Rasmussen crocheted. Dolores sat and watched Irving's cards change their minds from row to row.

A knock sent Irving to the door, a sigh from Mrs. Rasmussen's dry mouth, and animals to the edge of the cage inside Dolores.

It was Willie. Alone. He sang "Happy birthday, dear Dolores," like he was on the Arthur Godfrey Show, and set three packages on the table.

"Three," said Dolores.

"One from me, one from Ethel, and one from the blackberry vines."

Dolores laughed, "Jelly."

"Might be, might be. You just open and see."

"We'll have cake first," said Mrs. Rasmussen, "I'll go get it. Too blame bad Ethel can't be here to see it."

"Well, she's awful sorry," said Willie.

Dolores thought her mother was mad because Willie brought three presents.

Mrs. Rasmussen emerged from the pantry with a cake topped with green-dyed coconut. Stuck in the frosting was a set of her ceramic salt and peppers, a pair of blue jays; colored jelly beans clustered in the middle of the coconut. Seventeen candles ringed the cake. They had been lit before; Mrs. Rasmussen saved things that could be used again.

Irving struck a kitchen match and lit the candles; Dolores knew she had to try to blow them all out. Her breath threatened the flames. Her mother pinched out the ones left burning.

"Seventeen candles. Is that how old she's supposed to be?" asked Irving.

"That's supposed to be how many candles I could find in the drawer," and Mrs. Rasmussen pulled on the birds and cut into the cake.

Willie admired the recipe; Mrs. Rasmussen asked him to guess the secret ingredient. He tried milk.

"Lord, you can't talk to a man about nothin'. I sure wish Ethel'd come, too."

"Well, she's sorry she couldn't get over. I'll sure tell her how good this cake was."

"You'll take her a hunk. But that won't do no good for her to see how pretty it was."

"Pretty as a wedding cake," said Irving.

"Sure was a clever cake do," Willie affirmed.

"Dolores has got that recipe. I copied it off for her. It's pasted in her hope chest recipe book."

"How'd you like to meet a friend of mine, Dolores?" asked Willie.

"What?" frowned Irving.

"I got a friend who's comin' over tomorrow. He's sure the nicest guy. He's got a good idea, you know. He's a hard worker and besides he's started raisin' mushrooms in his basement."

"How can he tell if they're not toadstools?" asked Irving critically.

" 'Cause he grows 'em all himself. Then sells 'em to the big grocery stores."

"I'd never touch a mushroom with a ten-foot pole," said Mrs. Rasmussen, as though she were talking about whiskey.

Dolores knew that Willie was trying to talk about something else.

"Irving, why don't you and your sister come on over tomorrow about four?"

Irving caught on, "He got a wife?"

"Well, he had one. They're divorced."

"Never heard of such a thing," said Mrs. Rasmussen and laid a dish towel over the remaining cake like a shroud.

"Well, that woman he was married to, you never seen nothin' like it. She was so mean, Ben F would..."

"What's his name?" Dolores interrupted.

"Benjamin Franklin Gray."

"I heard of him."

"No, not that one. He's named for him. Well, anyway, Ben'd bring home his pay every week and she'd run off and buy canned hams and apple sauce and soda pop and take it all in Ben's station wagon to her relations. Ben couldn't keep ends meetin' 'cause she kept runnin' off and givin' everything away."

"It was family," protested Mrs. Rasmussen, her mouth drawn up like she had pulled a gathering string.

Willie paused. "Well, she was quite a good-sized, hefty woman. Seems she beat him up. He needs a real sweet-tempered girl."

They all looked at Dolores. "I'm going to bed," she said. "I've got a stomachache."

"Not from my tomato-soup cake, you don't. You sit here 'til you open your presents."

"That's okay," said Willie. "I got to be goin'. You open ours tomorrow. Then Irving'll bring you over about four, and you can tell Ethel if you liked 'em."

"She'll like 'em; she's learnin' manners," said Mrs. Rasmussen as though she were defending herself.

"You wear that pretty dress, Dolores."

"Tomorrow's not my birthday. It goes away."

"Yeah, but Ethel didn't get to see you in your dress, so you wear it for her." Willie waved to everyone and said good-bye as though they were across a field, and left back through the door with Ethel's piece of cake on a saucer. Dolores thought it might be hard for everyone to go visiting, not just for her.

"Open the presents," said Irving, putting his with Willie's.

"No, I'll do it tomorrow." Dolores went to her room and cried again.

She woke up before dawn and could think only of the presents on the kitchen table. She put on her slippers and went to get them. She was carrying them to her room when her mother said, "What are you doing up at this hour?"

Dolores was startled and dropped the packages. The blackberry jelly broke open and oozed out of the wrapping paper.

"Get back in bed. I'll clean this up. You can just wait a while since you wouldn't do it when you were supposed to."

Dolores waited. After she and Irving had their corn-flakes her mother gave her back the packages, minus the broken one.

"Where's the jelly?"

"Where do you think? It's gone. You can't eat broken glass."

Irving put his gift in her hands. She opened it. Blue Waltz perfume and barrettes in the shape of peacocks. They were painted an iridescent enamel.

"I like these best of all."

Her mother told her, "Hurry up and open the other two." One was a dishtowel embroidered with a kitten in a skirt, sweeping the floor.

"That's for your hope chest," said her mother.

The other package contained four large wooden rings. Too big for her fingers, too small for her wrists.

"Those are napkin rings. They're for your hope chest."

Dolores knew that all three of the hope chests were too full. She said to Irving, "The barrettes and this perfume is for me. Not for the hope chests."

Irving said, "I got to sharpen a cross-cut. It's gonna take me awhile," and he left.

Dolores performed her ritual, changing her padded cloth, wrapping it, burning it. Then she went back to her room. She wanted her bibs, but she didn't want to touch the swollen lid of the trunk. Once when she had been sick with the flu, she thought babies were in the trunk. She knew that was silly.

She stayed on the bed all day until her mother said, "You get ready now. But don't let no strange man touch you. They always try to touch girls like you."

Dolores put on her violet dress, some Blue Waltz, and the new barrettes. Her mother took out the barrettes, brushed her long wavy hair again, and reattached the peacocks where, she told Dolores, they belonged. "It won't be long now," said her mother.

Irving had put on a blue shirt that shined. He had combed his hair with water. Dolores saw little beads of water fall onto the shirt collar. It made him look sweaty, but he smelled cool.

"Let's go," he said. "Now, Dolores, don't try to say nothin' interestin'."

"Dolores," said her mother, "don't touch yourself and leave your hair alone."

"Do you want to put lipstick on her?" asked Irving, looking at her like one of his cards he called a one-eyed Jack.

"No. She looks younger without it."

Dolores started crying and cried so hard that Irving had to play solitaire while Mrs. Rasmussen applied cool washcloths to bring down the swelling. When she was ready Irving grabbed her wrist and pulled her out the door, letting some of his cards spill on the floor. Dolores saw her mother's black shoe step on one of the red face cards.

They went around the front way to Ethel and Willie's, where a station wagon with wooden doors was parked by the house. Dolores started to slow down, but Irving dug his fingers into her arm and pushed her toward the house. Ethel came out to meet them. "Oooh, you look pretty. My, you smell good, too."

"I gave her that perfume for her birthday," said Irving. They went into the house to meet the mushroom man. Dolores was trying to remember what that name was he'd been given.

"Well, hi, honey! Hi there, Irving!" Willie sounded like somebody was going to be Queen for a Day. "Glad you kids could stop over. Come on in the livin' room and meet a friend of mine."

Dolores liked the living room. All the furniture was fat and wore little crocheted doilies. It smelled like furniture polish and Ethel. The man stood up. He was short, pale, and seemed very clean; he had a large bald head. He looked like a mushroom himself, wearing gold-rimmed glasses. He looked out the window and down at the rug when he shook hands with Irving and nodded toward Dolores, matching the directions of their own nervous glances. Everyone stood like dancing bears waiting for the music to start until Ethel came in and put Dolores in a chair and then everyone else sat down. Ethel brought in a tray and put it on the coffee table.

"Well..." said Willie, beginning his sentence with the word that always seemed to make the others come after, "well, now, Ben F, tell us how you got started in that mushroom business."

Ben F's voice was high and light. "I guess whenever I went down in my basement the temperature and humidity always felt like the woods in the spring; and one day I said to myself, 'Boy, if I was a mushroom I'd love to be here.' So there was the idea."

Ethel, Willie, and Ben F laughed. Irving joined them. Dolores did, too, but just as everyone else was stopping. Hearing her voice alone in the middle of the room, she had to keep going, and asked the only question ready-shaped in her mind, "Did you always look like a mushroom, or just after you started growing them?"

Dolores didn't say anything after that. She felt what was happening as surely as Ben F had felt his mushroom enterprise. She couldn't eat her cookies or touch her coffee. She was afraid they'd spill. She traced the pattern of the rug with her eye until Irving pulled her out of the house, down the gully, through the blackberry bushes, and back to their house.

He was angry and began to tell their mother, "She acted like a moron. We just can't fool nobody with her. You shoulda been there. She..."

Dolores shut the door to her room so she wouldn't hear him. She decided to go to sleep and when she woke up it would be far from her birthday and people would leave her alone for awhile. Too many things had happened.

Dolores slept through to the next morning. She went out to eat her cereal. Irving was standing in the middle of the kitchen as still as she sometimes stood.

"She can't get up," he said. "I've got to go get somebody with a car. You help her."

When Dolores was little all the things that could hurt her or that she could ruin had been put in her mother's room and Dolores was not allowed to cross the threshold. And Dolores had never broken the rule, and the rule had never changed. But now Dolores went in. Her mother had wet the bed; she couldn't talk but in liquid sounds; it seemed she couldn't move. Dolores looked at her, touched her. Dolores finally realized that her mother couldn't get up and couldn't talk. She moved around the room where she'd never been. A place in her own house, strange and familiar. All the sewing things were there that her mother brought out every day and put back in the bedroom "so Dolores won't get ahold of anything and mess it up or hurt herself." Dolores picked up the scissors. Mrs. Rasmussen's noises increased. Dolores held out the lock of hair she'd been sucking and snipped it off. She let the scissors and the coil of wet hair fall into the basket of the threads.

On top of the dresser were objects that had never been carried into the other rooms. Dolores touched them. There was a dried-up starfish. She picked it up. She heard her mother on the bed, but Dolores had quickly come to know the powerlessness of this new mother as easily as she had known the power of yesterday's. But Dolores's eyes stopped at the mirror and met the angry reflection of the old woman behind her; still Dolores held on to the crusty starfish and noticed a few grains of sand had shaken from the center hole onto her palm. Her mother gurgled and Dolores held the starfish up to the mirror to blot out the old woman's reflection; the starfish hit the mirror and an arm cracked off and hit the dresser like chalk.

There was a picture of a man and a woman in a silver

frame. A wedding picture. It said "Dolores and John Rasmussen, 1917." She was confused until she realized that her mother's name had been Dolores when this picture had been taken.

There were too many things to see, so she left the room. She took the picture with her and set it on the kitchen table while she ate her cereal.

Irving came in with Ethel and Willie. "Look," she said, and held up the picture to them. They went past her without a word toward her mother's room. Dolores heard muffled sounds and guessed.

The last time Dolores saw her mother she had been turned into a waxed doll and laid in a satin-lined box. Dolores slipped the wedding photograph under the satin pillow, returning it to the first and former Dolores, drawing back before the lid might choose to fall and take her in, too.

Dolores didn't mind her mother's absence much. She wouldn't have liked it if it had happened before, but since she was going to be married before long, that's what her mother had said, then things would be different.

Willie had come over a couple of times and talked to Irving about red tape and paperwork. He didn't look at Dolores and say funny things to her; Dolores worried that he was mad at her.

Ethel came to ask her what she wanted to take with her. Dolores thought it was the marriage, coming at last. But everything Dolores suggested packing, Ethel would say, "Oh, honey, you won't need that. They'll have all that stuff."

"Is it the mushroom man?" Dolores asked.

"Sit down, sweetheart, let me tell you again, where you'll be."

Dolores forgot to listen because she saw that Ethel's wedding band was too small for her finger. The finger was pink and puffy around the ring. It looked like a little pig with a collar on too tight. "Does the ring hurt your finger?" Dolores wanted to know.

Ethel got up and went to the screen door, acting like she was looking in the yard, but her apron was crumpled against her eyes. Dolores thought she looked like the plump little animals embroidered on the hope chest dish towels and bibs.

Dolores went into her room and got her bibs out of the trunk. She knew these were the things she would take with her. She looked at the one with the duck carrying a basket of daisies. "When will it be my birthday?" she called out to Ethel.

Deer Crossing

THIS TOWN IS THE SCENE OF LOTS OF crimes, never suspected, never solved, never named. So you must wonder why everyone is after my sister Penny. Thanks for coming so far to look for clues. If I give them to you, maybe you can help get her free. She didn't murder anyone.

Yes, this is where we've lived since we were babies. Penny always says Deer Valley—like other towns named for the old inhabitants rather than the greedy latecomers— keeps waking to its ancient rhythms. She says everybody tries to resist that animal's heartbeat under the town's carpet of expansion. I think she's right. The town, she says to me, withstands the shadow of antlers that skims from the mountains down across our homes, the old railroad tracks, the river, the spire, the golden arches, the movie house, and the streets—named for presidents who never visited and for trees which don't grow in this climate. Penny says, like a historian, The tension of the town is ceremony criss-crossed with luxuriation, and she showed me how the heads of state go one way and the mother nature streets run counter.

There's a clue for you. The crimes are just evidence that the map of Deer Valley is raveling, unweaving itself by the force of the old heartbeat. Now it's the trout, more than the deer, who offer themselves up to welcome our travelers. Best fishing in the world, Frank always bragged, right along with the Chamber of Commerce.

This is not the beginning you asked me to start at, is it? Do you think now the Chamber of Commerce will start bragging that Penny is from Deer Valley and she's going to be a famous criminal? They'll never get the story right, though; they'll overlook the truth. It hasn't been easy for me to get the whole story in my mind. You wonder if there's any way to trace the story from its—well, not its beginning, but its—opening. I don't think so. We get the story first, then we find the clues we left dangling behind. That's the way stories go, the way crimes are solved, and that's the way the church runs it: first the body and blood, then the clues. I am giving you the clues.

My sister Penny's house is where Polk slashes through Eucalyptus. The porch runs along the house facing both streets. The name of the president implies, she said, that her place was not always great real estate. But poor old Lincoln is littered now with gas stations, fast food, parts and pipes. The tree name implies, she said, how hard our civilizers worked not to see what they already had. Pine, aspen, cedar, mountain ash, cottonwood, chokecherry, juniper are not in our directory of street names. But here they stand watch, and without them our secrets would dry up and blow free, Penny whispered once.

When Grandma died, I packed up and we took everything I wanted three blocks down Garfield, then over Teak, Avocado, Palm, Sycamore, Pomegranate, Olive, and Magnolia to Eucalyptus and into my sister's bridal house. Our grandma died, I got my first period, and Penny took me in, all in one week. Penny was more beautiful and more fun than I'd remembered from when she still lived with Grandma and me. Frank made more money than we would have guessed with his dad's hardware store; he was pretty nice to me when he was around. I waited awhile for Penny to have some babies, then forgot to expect them, just as she must have. There had been gossip that Penny was pregnant and desperate, so let this thirty-six-year-old man marry her. They thought the real father was Douglas, a cute guy killed on a rock climb at Maid of the Mist. Nobody guesses what's really going on. Penny said not even in Deer Valley these days does any woman think marriage is the answer to a surprise pregnancy. Or not many. Penny did carry on a lot when Douglas crashed down into Grayling Creek where the water's high and furious; but she was president of the Thespians then and I think she considered it her duty. Though maybe she really was suffering, because a long time ago Douglas had taught her how to french kiss before she ever needed to know. She showed me; I was just a little kid then and she said, Your tongue's like a rose bud. What about Douglas? I had asked. His was like a fish, she said. That's all she ever let him, nothing more. The real reason she rushed off to marry Frank was because she knew another child was coming: me. She knew Grandma would make it about one more year and she almost did. People still say Penny would have married Douglas, just took Frank out of grief and miscarried. But Penny knew all along who was going to step off a rock face and who was going to take over the family business, and she tried to provide what we needed. Now people say she caused Douglas to kill himself over Frank or maybe over Glenn. People have never been fair to her since she was in the fifth grade when Eddie Burns fell in love with her and watching her, ran smack in front of the pizza truck. Even after his concussion and broken leg, Eddie Burns still loved her, even until he got killed in his first car, driving it in the first snow. So no one forgave her. You can see that clue, I guess. Penny, they all thought, was guilty all along because she was always beautiful, amber-haired and big-eyed. Guilty all along, way before any crime. So, you see by the clues I'm showing you, Penny didn't commit any crimes; they all decided a long time ago that she's just guilty. When Eddie was hit, two pizzas slipped out the back of the delivery truck. Even the kids who ran off with the pizzas before the ambulance came never were easy on Penny. They weren't guilty. Penny was the reason the pizzas and Eddie were spilled out on the road.

No, I never went back to school after Grandma was gone. Penny called the principal, saying I was having a difficult grief and couldn't go back to class for the whole year. Jeannie's reading books, though, she reassured him. Mostly she was talking to me, trying to get me educated in a gentle way. Those first three years went by like a single spring, we were always in the mountains, and I never thought about school except once in awhile when we'd meet somebody who'd say, "How's school these days, Jeannie?" Penny taught me to say I never missed school. No one ever got our joke. It was a lame joke; we had to explain it to Frank. But Frank would say, "Anytime you want me to go down and get you enrolled, just say the word." I do re-member all the research Penny did to get letters sent to the school and to herself, really postmarked from Chicago, but she was the fake psychiatrist. She made me take achievement and aptitude tests and I'm always great on those synonyms, analogies, paragraphs, and all. Except, we had to sit down and do algebra and geometry workbooks. She made me shade in responses on lots of psychological tests where I admitted I have a good figure, or claimed I'd rather fly a plane than tend to plague victims. She said, Don't ever worry, Jeannie, I'll never force you to go to that school where they make you cry. Fly a plane or nurse plague victims, I'm glad I really don't have to choose between them.

At first she only let me read murder stories. The thing about them, Penny had said to me, is that when you can't stand to think about things like Grandma dying, or even

Douglas falling down the cliff, or way back to Momma and
Daddy being shot, you can read stacks of murder mysteries.
She told me she read them every day at the hospital, sitting
beside Grandma, watching over the liquids and the breaths
of her last week. Nothing like murder stories to keep your
mind away from death, Penny said. We lay in bed, reading.
She did most of the reading; I did most of the picnics and
manicures. She assigned me the mysteries, but she was on
to thick books which made her sigh and write notes in the
margins. Now Penny herself is a murder story, but her
formula's not quite working anymore. She can't keep us
from thinking about death.

We ordered silk pajamas from a catalogue. Penny's,
electric blue and mine, Chinese red. We did our makeup a
hundred ways. Frank said, "I know you feel bad, but if
someone stops by to pay respects, what'll they think?" People
didn't stop by. They paid their respects to Frank at the
hardware store as they picked out their brass fittings, hatch-
ets, and blenders, but they didn't come near us. Deer Valley
struggles to keep order above the heartbeat of the animal.
The hardware store provides them the means: mowers, drill
bits, sandpaper, cross-cuts, meat grinders, dimmer switches.
Screws, chains, rakes.

There are even simple clues in Deer Valley's little
changes, little cover-ups, little resistances. Penny notices.
Look, she said, that movie's called *She's Gotta Have It*. Mr.
Evans's marquee conceded to showing the movie, but spelled
out *She's Got To Have It*. There's a difference, Penny said,
and that's why he got the movie out of town in two days.
Mr. Carlsen got talked into a sign surrounded by flashing
lights for his appliance store. The salesman gave him a list
of amazing things to spell on his revolving marquee. Finally,
he sent his nephew up with the letters and had him print
"Maytag is a dependable value." Penny pointed it out to me,
the stodgy message he chose to put up in lights and scream
to all of Washington Street, all of Deer Valley. She likes to

laugh at Frank's Rotarians, as she calls them. See, they know they're contending with a force, but they have no idea where it's coming from. She said that about Father Keller, too, after she took the wafer and he looked at her. I don't put anything in my mouth or on my head from the church anymore. Penny says it's good not to do things that make me cry. So I don't take communion, cut up onions, think about Grandma, watch movies, or go to school. I could have graduated by now, so I think they've given up. Father Keller hasn't given up, but I won't talk to him, and I'm sure Penny's refusing to see him, too.

Once when my sister took me out hiking, and I gasped at the yellow and purple, she said, Be careful, don't look too intently. Not seeing is like forgetting, she said like a biologist, they are instincts of self-preservation. Can't blame the town for trying not to feel the heartbeat. Most people would go mad, she said, if they really saw a sunflower on the rocky side of the hill, let alone the clematis in the shade. Penny always sees, and she has always remembered. Do you think this is a clue? These clues are well below where the Inspector or the Old Lady would look. Once the horse from the pasture next to the cemetery was found in among the tombstones, and the horse skeleton from the biology lab was standing there too. That's a clue; no matter how industrious the Rotarians are, things break away.

Frank said, "Anytime you girls want me to do something about your Grandma's house, let me know." Later he said, "Don't let a good house sit empty too long." So we went down to go through it. There wasn't much we were interested in. Penny decided to take home an old secretary, the boxes of games, Grandma's thread and scissors. The rest we gave to the Help Center, and they delivered our secretary to us. Frank asked us if we wanted to sell or rent the house. We got out Grandma's Ouija board, which told Frank r–m–p–n–yes–s–l–h. He said, "Jeannie, you're still too young, but Penny, you should set an example. Be responsible." She did set an example. She made Frank get me a Gold Card like hers. They're intended for orphans, she said.

One dim, icy morning Frank cut himself shaving because Penny squirted his belly with shaving cream. When he sat at breakfast we admired his cut; Penny sighed and said, Don't you think now he looks like a brigand? I said he looked like a piggy bank with a slot in his cheek. He got up to go to work, and we drank red herb tea.

Who in Deer Valley would have found the clues before now? They were there, the momentum; but without the effect, no one discovers a cause leading to it. Penny took me up Kirk Hill. She was trying to point my head toward an oval hole in an aspen where she said a rouged baby woodpecker was pointing at us. Glenn passed us on the trail, then stopped and watched Penny swing over a log. Glenn was Frank's manager, and it seemed he was always around. Glenn looked, in the forest light, handsome and healthy enough to be an ad for something deadly, like cigarettes or whiskey. "Hi," he said. I know he went further into the forest; and I know he saw the harebells, forget-me-nots, shooting stars, strawberries, all in blossom. He went down the slope where the clematis were vining and pale trilliums were out. He saw patches of dogtooth violets. You can see this clue, can't you? Dogtooth violets are lilies, named to throw us off. Everything tries to hide, I said to Penny. Everything gives us clues, about themselves and about ourselves, she said. When we knelt to look at the dogtooth violets, Penny said all breathy and foxy, See, Jeannie, their yellow silk petals curl back and they flaunt their velvet vermilion trembling sex. And then she laughed. There was a shadow, a snap, and a hush; I thought Glenn was listening to her. Maybe it was the deer, though. I liked to carry bouquets home. They're too fragile, she'd tell me. But I took them anyway.

Penny would never pick a flower. It's not murder, I defended myself; they still have their roots and it doesn't kill the plant, it's fine. Well, Penny said, it's like punching a pregnant woman in the stomach, picking a flower is causing a plant abortion. I still picked them. So she got me a flower presser with little wing nuts, a bunch of thick paper, and spray-on glue. And, once I had all that equipment, she knew I'd leave the flowers where they were in the hills. I still don't think it's bad to pick a flower. Penny said, No, Jeannie, it's fine, if you really want to; I just stopped doing those things myself. I thought she meant picking flowers, though don't you believe the clue is really that she had stopped giving herself abortions?

But I don't think she's ready to be a mother, except to me. And, I guess she's been Mother since we lost ours. I was too young to remember anything about the time in the car when they were killed, except the sound, and my mother's final spreading, wet gesture as she spun back toward her babies, who were safe but dappled with parental blood. Another of Deer Valley's crimes, unsolved. I used to dream of this valley full of gliding deer and parents, hunted, then extinguished. Penny told me once years ago when I cried too much, that the same thing happened to the president, a long time ago, back when presidents were like statues and gardens. He was riding in a car, too, and his wife was wearing pink, just like us, and she was spattered with his blood and brains, just like us. Penny has always wanted to comfort me the only way she knew, to stroke my eyes closed, to unbind my thoughts. Penny says no one found out whether our parents were shot by the random or by the intentional. Even Frank said that the local rifle club got national instructions and money to help get the story quickly forgotten. The only ones who seem to remember what happened to our folks are the ones who are afraid we're trying to get guns outlawed.

One day we went down to Frank's store and looked at all the sports equipment. Frank said, "You girls don't have much use for these things, you're pretty hale and hearty,

but you can have one machine if you want it." Penny folded
her arms across her peasant blouse, concentrating on
whether we wanted the rowing machine or the stationary
bicycle, and wadded the cotton together with her fingernails
and pooched her lip. The blouse slipped off her shoulders
and Frank blushed. He said, "Just go on home, I'll have it
delivered." Glenn brought over five machines that afternoon,
a whole workout gym. He set it all up while we tried the
equipment in our glitter tights. He watched through his
eyelashes. He had to come back the next day to finish.

A couple of weeks later Frank asked us how the exercise
was going and Penny asked him for some stuff to refinish
the secretary. Frank was pleased. "It's cherry," he said. Glenn
brought by the supplies and explained all the dangers to
Penny's hair, her t-shirt, the space behind her. When we
pulled out the drawers we found an old studio photograph
of a man resting his hand on a fringed tablecloth. It looks
like the palm tree is sprouting from his head, we said. This
is Gabe, said Penny and pretended to have heard all about
this secret man Grandma must have loved. His eyes were
black, bold; his fingers spread and caught seductively in the
fringe; his hard, lean hips were tensed, ready, Penny purred.
We laughed; I was glad she had stopped making me read
the mysteries and thought I was well enough for some with
guys with black, bold eyes. It was then she tried to start
me on Ovid and Augustine, but we spent more time with
the photograph.

Penny said he was a Rampant Soul, bounding from
one animate body to another, until he came to reside in
Gabriel just at the moment he met my grandmother, wasp-
waisted and her hair loosening from the combs. I don't
know whether Penny made this story up, read it someplace,
or if it's something Grandma told her. How could Grandma
have lost Gabriel to cardboard and the back of a drawer?
Penny said, Remember when Grandma used to rock us on
the porch when the weather was changing mood? She'd let

her sorrow show and we'd watch the clouds roll over the valley. Grandma told us, "Watch them split open, revealing their silver linings to us." Those silver linings, Grandma said, "they show themselves, but stay safely, ever, beyond our reach." However it happened that Penny came by the story of Gabriel, the Rampant Soul, she wouldn't let go of it; she told me chapters every time I turned around. I came to love Gabe, too. We were devoted to him, to his Rampant Soul. We bought him candles at Hallmark's. Penny got him a cherry-scented angel because she said that's how Grandma ended up. Waxy and stiff, I added. We laughed to show each other we didn't take this stuff too seriously. I had learned to be normal about people dying and Penny said those murder stories had been my therapist. I don't remember finishing many of them. To be able to move calmly among the corpses is, as far as Penny was able to find in her reading, one of the tests of sanity. Whose? I bought Gabe three floating duck candles for the bathtub. If you think ordinary men are hard to buy for, Penny laughed, try buying for the disembodied man, for a Rampant Soul. Candles seemed to be all Gabe would want, though Penny liked to read, she said, to both of us.

A Rampant Soul, she explained, loses its bodily life in the midst of ecstasy. Ever after that, the Rampant Soul, like a deer raised up on its hind legs, a rare sight, travels from body to body, exchanging and discarding them as it goes, snuffing them out, because it can't find one afire with that ecstasy. Could Grandma once have had charm or fire enough to compel the Rampant Soul? That last lonely year after Penny's lily and honeysuckle wedding, I remember Grandma's hand hovering over things without being able to close around them. One time, she reached for a potato I was supposed to peel, which I had laid on the shelf alongside the tea boxes. The potato had sprouted, as Penny said—even though she hadn't been there with Grandma and me—a long tendril, two vernal leaves, and Grandma suddenly wept to see that single potato, displaced, withering, but surging with a futile, new life. "What is the Resurrection," Grandma had cried, "if the earth shrinks beneath it?" I tried to put my arms around her, but she didn't know me, couldn't feel me, then. "The grave collapses and swallows up the renewed body. Again. If you can rise again, who's to say you can't die again?" Grandma did not sound as if she were someone who had met up with a Rampant Soul. She was accusing her final companion, Penny said, tangling with death. Even the stories I tell to Penny, she tells them back to me, better. Can't I just visit her now for a little while?

We filled fruit jars with branches of lilacs, set them in every room, on the stairs, even on the washer. Frank joked, "It's like a funeral." We couldn't tell him Gabe adores the house filled with lilacs, everyone faint with the scent. Penny asked me to remember the Polaroid camera she had given me, that first year we were with Grandma without Daddy and Momma. Jeannie, we took you out to Grayling Creek and Elk Springs and you used all your film on two identical Deer Crossing signs. Do you remember? She told me I took the pictures home and lined them up on the rug. Yellow board with black, silhouetted, leaping deer. No people, no scenery, Penny laughed; it's as though we didn't get the point until now. Penny understood my Polaroids as a clue. You see, she said, European heraldry depicts lions and unicorns as rampant—raised on their hind legs. You can imagine that sometimes I wished she were not so responsible about my education. But the road sign is, she said, a rampant deer, a herald of the Rampant Soul, and I had discovered it when we were so young. Penny has always given me credit for unusual insights.

She took me up into the Badger Mountains and we found, under a giant fir, a cushion of star moss, ornamented with violets and thimbleberries. This is the deer's bed, I told Penny. We curled up there, trying it out. As we left, Penny said with a little catch of regret, I hope he delights in our scent. You see, everything had already happened.

Then the rain came, hard, wrecking our fall leaves, closing the house around us, graying the air. Penny went soft. Thunder mumbled across the roof, and then glass shattered, and we heard the animal. When I went downstairs I could smell the rain and the goat. The dining room window was broken and a goat, all knotted up in ropes, was peeing on the rug. He looked like a goat in a doily, it had been tied so many times.

Frank said, "I don't understand why this would happen three weeks before Halloween." He couldn't see it as anything but a mean trick-or-treat, so he'd have revised the calendar before he'd have changed his mind. He decided to take the goat out to his dad's place. "Don't wait up. I'll stay and have breakfast with Dad, then go to work from there." He taped plastic over the window and said he'd send Glenn over to fix it in the morning.

Was this just what Glenn had planned? Frank was so predictable, the only thing he'd think to do with a goat was take it to his dad's in the country. Long as he was there, he'd stay, have breakfast, and go straight in to work. So at first I thought it was Glenn's doing, but Penny was certain it was a Rampant Soul's joke.

Penny dumped a box of baking soda on the rug and went back to bed. She wasn't scared or curious. It wasn't a clue, only for Frank, a false clue tumbling him toward his end, nothing more. As I turned out the hall light, I saw Penny step out of her nightgown and throw herself on the bed; she was waiting for the flashes of lightning to give her glimpses of her photograph of Gabe. So when Glenn climbed up over the porch, ripped the window screen, and stood over her, she handed him the photograph. Lightning made the shadow of the branches outside and of the man in her room spring together across the wall and ceiling. Penny gazed at the tree-man's trajectory through her room, and she welcomed his flesh into her bed.

Detectives aren't smart, just lucky, Penny says. She says criminals leave them strings of clues: plaster busts, musical boxes, the cigars of connoisseurs. Anyone can solve crimes if the criminals are so obliging and the investigator so lucky. If you have only rope, candlestick, revolver, lead pipe to choose from, you don't have to do the difficult work of finding out what might be a clue. Clues, she says, will not come so straight. Deduction—as well as induction—only works if everyone's in the same system. Miss Scarlet, Professor Plum, or the Ballroom; suspects, as well as conditions, are also clues. In my home education, Penny says she doesn't want me to be fooled by the irrational desire for reason or tidiness. Frank gave me a kitten and Penny named him Logo so everyone would hear it as Loco. I can explain why she thinks it's funny, if you want. She's always had a lot of laughs, being my whole school. She likes to read. Can I take some of her books to her, at least? Maybe I should just take her the old murder stories; she might be frightened, locked up until bail is set on Monday. My kitten disappeared; I don't think Frank liked it. Logo had worn a long-distance look, so Penny and I placed ads in out-of-state newspapers. Three cats were shipped to us on the Greyhound. Two of them came with names, regular names, Anthony Quinn and Charles. So, Penny said I had to name the third one. None of the cats fit the description of Logo, not one with white socks; Charles has little gray slippers. Close enough? What were the clues people used, to link these cats to our ad? Not color, size, or name. Now you see how things work.

What did I name her? Well, she was the third cat to arrive. Frank got tough then and said, "Too many damn cats. She has to go to the Humane Society." So I named her Frank and gave her a good-bye party.

Oh, yes. Well, three weeks later, and this time Frank was right, it was Halloween, a harvest moon. The newly replaced window shattered again, and suddenly the room was filled with magpies. Frank worked the rest of the night trapping birds; and I heard Glenn come through the upstairs window again. Frank the cat would have been quicker at grabbing the magpies.

After that, after Glenn thought he had Penny's attention, he didn't work so hard to distract Frank's, if it was Glenn and not the Rampant Soul having fun. Go for the simplest answer, right? That always makes Penny laugh. Frank and Glenn were buddies; they decided together that Anthony Quinn should come and live in the stockroom in the basement of the store. So we were down to Charles. He came to us clear from Sedona, Arizona, and we didn't even advertise for Logo in that state. Charles is wonderful. He always senses the presence of the Rampant Soul. It's not irrelevant. Charles is a suspect, isn't he? Like that big hound out on the moor.

Okay. A few days after Christmas, we found Frank's body at the bottom of the stairs. I carefully covered any marks on the baseboards and stair railings where wire might have been attached to trip him; I poured out all his liquor, just in case of poison; and to help the police out, I put empty bottles of all our medication in his nightstand, if he might have, or should have, overdosed. Penny gracefully made arrangements, just as she had for Grandma. Frank, they said, had died from a sudden heart attack; they blamed Penny for that, too. You can guess what they said, you don't want me to repeat it. Young, passionate bride stuff. They said they felt sorry for her, too, but anybody with so much bad luck is going to come in for a lot of blame.

I suppose you think Glenn killed Frank. All the motives are there, but none of the real clues. If there were any, I cleaned them up.

Spring came round again. Look closely, Jeannie, figure it out, Penny was always saying, Have you ever noticed that flowers spend so much of their vital energy being beautiful?

Sure, I said. But, she said like a secret, flowers don't have eyes. They can't see one another, blossoms have no mirrors. Don't forget that, she said; moreover, they expend vital energy on scent, but they have no noses. Flowers who can make our knees buckle with their aromas, did not bother to develop nostrils. They can't even sneeze from their own pollen, I added. Most people, Penny said, care only that flowers have no legs, though in two seasons they can cover a hillside. Locomotion of flowers is a false issue, plants standing still, animals moving. That's not the big clue about flowers. Yes, I asked, but is that how they save themselves, preserve themselves, by not seeing? Not remembering? If they knew how they look, how they smell, they'd go crazy. And how, asked Penny, laughing, would a mad flower behave? I was going to say, like a bee, but she put a stone in my mouth, to teach me mineral silence.

Glenn tried to get Penny to move to Mahogany Street, just off Cleveland. Glenn said I could live with them, too, but I'd have to go back to school. We like it on Polk and Eucalyptus. So, Penny said she'd marry him in a couple of years if he agreed to keep his own place and visit us only when she invited him. He was pretty interested in the hardware store by then, so he stayed on Mahogany except when Penny was in the mood for cooking or whatever. I don't think she liked him after he started walking in by the door, just like Frank had done, talking taxes and inventory.

One day Penny told me Glenn called and was taking us to lunch. We drove eighty miles to a restaurant; I thought then that they were running out of ways to have fun. The waiter brought Glenn white toast instead of whole wheat, so he ate Penny's croissant. Then when he finished his lunch, he piled most of Penny's chicken salad on his white toast and ate that. Gestures of ownership, Penny said and smiled when she saw I noticed. Penny's so beautiful, though, you'd wonder what it's all for, not for Frank or Glenn to own her, but for the Rampant Soul to find her.

On the way home, I slept in the back of the car and listened to them a little. I was right about the toast; Penny was feeling smothered. Sometimes men are most smothery when they're focusing on a distance, unaware of the life they're crushing, Penny once said. It was fall again, and Penny had to make one of her trips to the high school, carrying her official-looking files that show how I'm too nervous or something to go to school. Glenn was fixing our disposal I had crammed full of spinach leaves. "You look great," he said, "you just like to play hooky." He said I ought to go to school, chased me around the house, told me what the high school boys were missing. I threw dishes at him. He told Penny that she was right, I had fits or something, was paranoid. She finally told him, Glenn, I am sometimes visited by a Rampant Soul. He is the one I love, not you.

When Glenn killed himself, I put on rubber gloves and set out little suicide objects in both the Mahogany and the Eucalyptus houses. I laid Glenn's gun on his couch, put Easter stickers like kisses along the barrel; I put a rope in his closet, with the light on, so its shadow swung over his bed. In our house, I put rat poison—no, not in the cookie jar—in the ice cube tray. But that wasn't a very good idea; I got rid of it. I put knives pointing up in the dish drainer; I spilled bath oil on the tile; I laid a hose across his Pontiac. Once again, I helped the police with things so they'd have something to write on their clipboards. Accident, suicide, or murder. Actually, I don't know how Glenn did it. He did it down in the stockroom; I guess Anthony Quinn was the first to find him. If Anthony Quinn is not implicated. The police are keeping the details to themselves. There might be evidence the Rampant Soul did him in; the police would suppress that. You can see that Glenn had every reason to kill himself, though you couldn't say he had any motive for it. A hardware store, when it comes right down to it, is a big collection of murder and suicide ideas.

Do you think there are clues I'm not seeing, or clues I've forgotten? When they came to get Penny, the lilacs were shedding their four-point blossoms all across the walk, like heaps of tiny rusted crosses. Spring is drying up, blowing, free.

So you see, it's really too late for me to go to school, I don't feel the need. Penny has seen to it that I've read the classics, the Constitution; she taught me biology and logic. Now we will study law. She's a young, beautiful widow. Encumbered, as I heard her say, with a big hardware store. We might move to Chicago, where all those letters were postmarked. Or, we might go visit the man in Arizona who sent us Charles. You can't help her, you just want the clues. I would help her if I could; but if I confess to the crimes, then she'll confess to them in order to save me. You know they'd believe her over me. The only way to help is for all of us to be innocent. And there's a Rampant Soul free, in this valley, and wanting her, too, to be free.

Margaret
of the
Imperfections

MARGARET FAVORED HER LEFT FOOT
as she walked up the hill toward her house, which from
some angles looked about to collapse into accordion pleats
down the hill and into the sea, but from other angles appeared to be squatting, ready to leap into the sky. Left by
her grandfather's death, the house and Margaret protected
each other from abandonment. Margaret had become a
woman there, but like her house, seemed precariously
perched between disengaging herself from the world or
disassembling herself in it. Her sudden limping set the
rhythm of her return, the curves of her body gave in to
angular notions of pain, all counterpointed by the wind in
the waves of her hair.

She opened the door of her house, the late yellow light
on the pink walls resembled the interior of an illuminated
shell; and like a simple organism of mere panicked flesh,
she retreated into it. She took off her shoe and discovered
a small white growth on the side of her little toe. Before
she went to sleep she wondered whether it was an irritation

to the surface of her skin or a more ominous eruption from within.

That night she dreamed the rose vines on the pink wallpaper in the hall crawled out into all the rooms and exploded into blossom. The people from the town were at the windows, reaching for roses. The vines were tearing at Margaret's clothes; the sweet scent was suffocating her when she escaped back into wakefulness. Her toe was throbbing and the little growth, enlarged to the size of a blackberry, looked exactly like a pearl. Margaret touched it; it was cool. She tugged at it and the pearly knob fell into her hand. An iridescent circle like a fish scale remained on her toe, and Margaret wept.

Several days went by; her health remained firm but her purse collapsed. Margaret no longer worked at the inn, playing the flute, serving soup, peeling vegetables, and smiling at her suitors' attempts to entangle her in their conversations. But her pursuers, Harold and George, had wearied of being rivals and became collaborators, plotting together to force her to make up her mind between them.

"I'll choose neither of you; I'll live alone," she had said, and let them watch her scrub the carrots.

So they had brought the innkeeper into the game and Harold suggested that if Margaret should lose her job, she would be forced to choose a husband to provide for her. George offered the innkeeper a pregnant mare if he saw to it that no one else in the town offered her a position while they waited for her to decide.

But Margaret had filled up her days going to the church in the middle of the town, to the sea at its edge, and back to her house at the top of the hill. She crocheted lace for the priest's sleeves and traded clams for apples. She played with the children, gossiped with the wives and old men, and watched the tide bring her gifts and erase her footprints.

Charley the slow-witted boy, happiest for Margaret's unemployment, sat every day in the dusty road, building a model of the city from bits of wood, broken glass, and colored tin, turning the town to his own design. He made a castle that didn't exist and left out the school. Margaret brought him tide treasures for his city; some he threw aside, others he washed with his tongue and made part of his microcosm. Margaret saw that her own house came to be represented by the best tin box, and the surrounding adornments of broken glass and marbles grew to dwarf and shame the rest of the village.

And the ideal city affected the mundane one it arose in. The priest and the innkeeper had attempted for two years to move Charley's venture to a backyard or even to the churchyard. But Charley would return to the spot that seemed to him the only place in their world where he might create his own. Finally, the oldest woman in town forced the priest and the innkeeper to attend only to what they could control. So instead of attempting to displace an idiot boy, they hired workers to widen the road, and the town in some small way was actually reshaped by Charley's imagination of it.

Charley was retracing the passageways of his structure when Margaret brought her pearl to town. She bent and offered the pearl to him. He looked at it, took it, put his tongue to it, shook his head, and returned it to her. Since the pearl had no place in Charley's architecture, Margaret put it in her pocket and went to see Albert the red-bearded jeweler and wood-carver. The pearl was as cool as a dog's nose in her pocket.

Albert squinted at it, tasted it as Charley had, and offered Margaret money for it, more than she ever would have earned at the inn.

"Are you sure it's real? I found it in the drawer of my grandfather's old smoking stand," she lied. "I just wondered if it's real."

"It's real. It's a natural, South-sea white."

Margaret took the money and wondered whether she

should confess avarice or pride. She gave a considerable portion of it to Charley, a smaller portion to the church. Charley used his in the stonework of his miniature church, but the other boys saw it and took it from him.

Charley was the child of a widow who had died of influenza; only the priest knew who his father was. Father Thomas kept his own genealogical records in a secret book. Years ago the priest had heated a silver letter opener in a candle flame and inscribed on the leather cover, *Book of Fathers*. The pages were nearly filled with children's names, baptisms, and the narratives of mothers conjoining with unacknowledged fathers. "The records are necessary," Father Thomas had said, "to protect the town by preventing an inadvertent sin of incest. The devil draws us to our own. Incest is the sin of lust throwing up a mirror before the sin of pride." He had used his insight as a sermon once, but the men slept and the women planned their dinners. Both Charley and Margaret were the objects of extended narratives in Father Thomas's book of bastards.

On the way home Margaret bought pears, walnuts, and wine for Harold and George's evening visit.

They were not pleased with her display of wealth and resolved to watch her more closely. Nevertheless, they persisted in their rituals of courtship, measuring their potential solemnity by their current wit, their amorous levity a projection of the future marital gravity.

George pretended to pluck the sound from the tines of a silver fork with his fingernails and drop the ringing into the wine or make it bounce off the table. His square, hairy paw hid the handle of the fork and the secret of the sound. George even dropped the reverberation down the front of Margaret's dress, saying, "A ring for you." She blushed, looked down, and saw a small pearl on her left breast, half hidden in the lace. She spilled her wine; they teased her and mopped it up.

George taught her how to perform the trick—letting

Margaret pluck the fork tines and pretend to hold the ringing in her fingers and then surreptitiously touching the handle of the fork to the oak table at the right moment, making the persistence of the sound waves audible again and pretending to fling sound against the walls or George's knee. They laughed until George touched Margaret's right elbow and it tingled. She drew away. She felt a hard lump there and fell silent.

Harold then took his fountain pen and paper from his vest pocket. He grinned and quickly outlined what looked like a Christmas tree standing behind several spirals. "Well," he challenged, "what is it?"

"Christmas cur'ls?" asked George.

"No," glared Harold. There was silence again.

"Three turtledoves, two french hens, and a partridge in a pear tree!" exclaimed Margaret stupidly.

"No, dear," snorted Harold, "it's swirls before pine."

Margaret burst into tears. George and Harold washed her dishes, kissed her chastely, and walked down the hill together in the darkness, making sympathetic sounds for whichever of them should be the winner. A woman after all, they agreed, was an ambivalent creature, an ambiguous prize, yet each thought more ardently of winning Margaret for himself.

In her little bedroom painted blue over the cut-out animals glued on in her childhood, Margaret forgot to see the blue before her, but out of habit recalled the old images now obscured. Undressing before her hidden beasts, she discovered the worst. The pearl on her elbow was large, baroque; the one she had noticed under the lace of her neckline had become a fairy ring of small pearls around her left breast. There were five pearls constelled on her pale belly, three behind her right knee, one where her anklebone protruded. Margaret twisted them off, leaving the fish-scale marks on her skin, and cast them into the lacy heap of her underclothes on the floor.

Margaret dreamed of a man who kissed her; he had a mole on his neck that was a faceted ruby. When she awoke she longed for the man, but she knew that men didn't really grow rubies and she was alone in the world. She had developed seven new pearls along her thighs. She left them until the afternoon when one had increased to the size of a grape; she plucked them off.

She found her mother's embroidered bag and gathered all the pearls into it, and holding the drawstring bag in her lap, she remembered her mother's delight with the rich indigo color. The last memory, and the first, that Margaret held of her mother was woven into the purse. Margaret had been four when her mother was commissioned to embroider something for the church, Margaret didn't remember what. She did remember her mother giggling, snipping off the end of the holy cloth for her own purse. Margaret had stood by her mother's chair, bare feet swathed in the abandoned fabric, and watched an angel worked in chain stitches. As Margaret now pressed her finger against the angel's garment, she heard her mother saying then, "Angels don't go to church." "Neither does Grandfather," Margaret had said. "Grandfather's rebelling," she laughed, "angels have outgrown that; they just play." "Do angels grow?" "No, they pretend to outgrow things; they play." Her mother had made vines for three days, with three seasons of green. Margaret had watched her mother thread the purple and give the angel grapes, and she had watched her thread the silver and give the angel jackstones. When Margaret had gone to bed that night her mother was threading pink and giving the angel roses. But her grandfather told her the next morning that her mother had drowned in the sea. The priest came; Margaret thought he wanted the purse so she sat on it while he talked about defying the Will of Heaven until her grandfather told him to leave. After that she remembered her grandfather teaching her to forgive the sea and the priest teaching her to say her rosary.

The pearls stirred within the bag and Margaret, looking

at the silver crosshatches, suddenly realized that her mother had meant the jackstones to be stars, and after all these years she saw the intended stars.

She went to the priest that afternoon and confessed the pearls. Father Thomas had stealthily provided Margaret his natural paternity but openly offered her fatherhood only in its ecclesiastical form. She didn't know; he sometimes forgot. But there were three or four in the town who looked upon Margaret as a celestial gift to them, conceived as she had been in the glow of consecrated wine beneath the wooden gaze of the Virgin.

"I had a dream once," she confided rather than confessed, "that I called you Dad instead of Father. And you called me Mollie, my mother's name."

"The Blessed Virgin once wept pearls."

"It's not the same. They were the perfection of her sorrows. These come in unexpected places, for no reason."

"If they come at all, God has a reason."

"A punishment, Father, to display my imperfection? Or a gift to earn me a living?"

"To reveal to you who you are." The priest was trembling. "Go home, Margaret."

That evening Margaret played her flute, served poppy-seed cake and port, and announced to her suitors that she was turning their game around; she had riddles for them.

"This is the first riddle. You must guess," she smiled, "which of you will give me up when I ask you my next riddle."

"The one who doesn't love you," George responded quickly.

"Too easy," countered Harold. "It will be the one who doesn't love riddles."

"You both guessed the first. Now here is the second." Margaret lifted her green velvet dress and turned her leg. "Why is it that I grow pearls?" She let the shawl slip from her shoulders. "Twenty-one yesterday, only eleven today."

The three were silent a while, roused by port, flesh, pearls, and new ideas.

"They're real," she said. "Albert buys them." She began to break them off like random barnacles, and drop them on the carpet before them.

"That doesn't prove they're real," said Harold. "A real pearl comes from an oyster in the sea. These only seem to be pearls. They're a disease. Their source is to be found in the foods you eat or the thoughts you have."

"Ah, but that means the source is the same. The oyster," explained George, "is troubled by a grain of sand and makes a pearl to comfort itself. Margaret is troubled by something, too, and thus is producing pearls."

"I am troubled only by pearls," Margaret interrupted. "It's not a disease. It's an error, a flaw. A mistake in the design of me but not something gone wrong with some part of me. I was certain to give off pearls; it was inevitable. The pearls are not an accident, nor a punishment, nor a plague. You cannot answer my riddle." She gathered the shawl to her neck, lowered her skirt, and told them good night.

As the two suitors descended the hill George said, "I'll keep her, Harold, I don't mind a woman who's deformed; the value of the pearls will make up for it."

"On the contrary," said Harold, "it makes a plain woman more exciting. I'll take her."

"So, she still has the two of us to choose from." And they sent their sighs toward the scattered stars and walked along the beach.

"Margaret will never choose," Harold decided, "as long as we continue to court her so well."

They sat on the sand, tossing pebbles into the tide. "She has no motivation to change things as they are. We must court another woman to stir her up a bit."

"Yes! That's it. We'll ignore Margaret and deflect our affection for her onto another."

"How about Millicent? Young widows are said to be

passionate; she is certainly more beautiful and wealthier than Margaret. It's believable enough."

"But Millicent is the only woman in town," Harold grumbled, "who never feeds Charley."

"She made him a shirt last winter, from her dead husband's."

"Then she'll do," he said with a grunt of enthusiasm.

And they began to court Millicent. Margaret made no mention of the apparent shift of affection. She continued to play with Charley, confess and pray, speak to the sea, and pry off her pearls.

"In the darkness, Father, it felt like rippling water washing through, swelling the house, and the house pressing it out and down the hill, and I touched myself."

The priest began to measure out the penance, but Margaret interrupted, "Wait, Father, wait." It was as still as an eavesdropping angel. "When I touched myself—"

"That's enough, child. Don't add on the sin of turning the confessional into your dream theater."

"Father! Wait. When I touched myself I felt little ridges of pearls like the silver beadwork on the chalice. They're there, too. Pearls. Like sweet, round teeth, like a mouth, like the edges of a shell, they fit together like . . ."

But Father Thomas stopped her gathering momentum and set her to praying.

Margaret prayed and sold her pearls.

Albert the jeweler drilled holes in the pearls, strung them and sold them to Harold, who gave them to Millicent. Millicent wore them to church, elegant against her widow's black. Harold and George looked at Millicent and thought about Margaret. Margaret looked at her pearls.

"Those are my pearls," she hissed, "I recognize them."

After mass George said to her mildly, "They look better on her than they did on you."

"Millicent, indeed, is a lovely woman, perfectly decorated," added Harold.

"Why on me," asked Margaret shrilly, "were they a flaw, a grotesquerie, mistaken for disease, and on her a tribute to her beauty?"

"They're not a disease," Harold patronized her, "you're right about that. You go on making pearls; we'll go on seeing Millicent. It's a woman's obligation to wear pearls well, a man's to bring them to her. Where does a woman who grows pearls fit in to the order of things?"

They nodded to Margaret and escorted the widow home. But Margaret noticed that Harold glanced at George and George glanced back to Margaret, and Margaret, looking past them toward the sea, understood their game again.

Margaret waited until the moon was shrouded and crept into Millicent's house. She found her way to the widow's bedroom and hardly considered who the heavy snorer next to Millicent might be, as she sought the pearls. There on the dresser, they looked like an exotic serpent escaping their satin envelope.

Millicent turned over in bed and flung an arm across the bestial sleeper next to her, raised up, still asleep, and said, "Come what may." Margaret recognized dreamers for what they were, but hurriedly backed out of the room. It seemed that the pearls clanked like a chain. "Someone's there!" shouted the dreamer, waking the man, who stumbled naked and erect to the kitchen where Margaret hid.

She grabbed the circular stove lid by the lifter and held it before her like a shield. The man felt hot metal knock against his knees and elbows; his dragon deflated and he fled back to Millicent's arms. They shivered until dawn and discovered in the thin light that the demon had left black, sooty marks on the man which had rubbed off on Millicent.

Margaret had thrown the stove lid into the crockery and raced down the dark road only to trip on Charley's tin and wooden city. His castle and sailboat punctured her palms, making them bleed. Her dress tore and she was cut under her breast by the house he called Margaret's. The pearls unstrung and scattered into configurations in the dust, mocking the stars in the sky.

Crawling on her hands and knees as to stations of pilgrimage, she gathered each pearl and lifted it to the light that wasn't there. When she finished she had 173 pearls. "Four of them, or at least three, are impostors," she thought. She carried them in her left shoe and hobbled with one bare foot in the Prussian-blue wash of the sky that comes before morning, toward the church. It began to rain.

Margaret entered the church like a shadow. She dipped her fingers into the hot wax of the votive candles before the image of the Virgin and used the wax to affix the pearls and the three pebbles and the marble she'd inadvertently gathered with them, to the hem, the belly, the thighs, the wrists, the breasts, the hair, the graceful neck, even the cheeks, of the statue. Some of the last pearls, the first gathered, were tinged by the blood from her hands, and they lent a blush to the Virgin's cheeks.

Margaret sat down on the floor and, now oblivious to the beaded statue, began to peel the wax from her fingers.

"Margaret," said a voice behind her.

"Father."

"So you know," he said, thinking of himself.

"Yes," said Margaret, thinking of Heaven.

Her dress was damp and wadded into her lap, her thighs the palest light in the church. "I could have mistaken you for your mother," he said, wondering if all the pearls were gone as he reached toward her.

"Don't touch me." She picked at the wax droplets congealed on her cheek.

"I had prayed for a son," he said.

"The rain will stop soon," she answered.

"But I fathered a saint; a sin engenders purity. How can I interpret the Gospel for my children now? Now that I have gained knowledge and lost understanding?"

Margaret didn't listen to the man who had seeded her mother.

"Margaret. Your mother was as dim as Charley; your father's sin was to betray the innocent. I will be flung to the core of hell with the traitors, while she dully embroiders on its hem. And, yet, from this comes a saint. Why is the pure repellent? Why do I shrink from it?"

She knew he had misread her mother. She challenged, "How can the pure be a flaw pressed into the world?"

"Margaret, the pearls are signs. You are one of God's saints."

"I'm not even very good, Father."

"Saints often aren't. They are simply those that are neither in this world nor beyond it, touching the holy and being touched by it."

"I can't be a saint. I dreamed Charley was the priest. It was a funny dream and I laughed for days."

"You are touched by sainthood. I don't know what to do. The Pope will have to be informed. The inquiries will begin; the burden of you is greater than I can bear."

"Don't worry, Father. No one will find out. I'll get married. All this will perish. I'll marry George and have children by Harold. Or, the other way round; offer me to anyone you will, or to the first who comes to confess. I'll have one child by Albert. You won't know which. And we'll watch them, Father, you and I, only the two of us, to see if this cursed gift will continue into the world, if the saint can give birth to bliss, to greatness, or to goodness or even to hope. Or will the children, Father, be indistinguishable from the others? And might that, Father, be the sign after all?"

Margaret departed, leaving her shoe at the Virgin's feet, a damp spot at the priest's.

When she came to Charley's devastated city, she wrote to him with a stick on the road, *I love you Charley. We will make the city again.* She remembered then that Charley couldn't read, but he'd know it was from her and he'd know its meaning.

She went home and bathed. Her scales, where the pearls had emerged, fell off and floated in the bathwater and drained into the sea.